os

Careers in Focus
GERIATRIC CARE

SECOND EDITION

GERIATRIC CARE

SECOND EDITION

Ferguson

An imprint of ☑®Facts On File

Careers in Focus: Geriatric Care, Second Edition

Copyright © 2005 by Facts On File, Inc.

Ferguson
An imprint of Facts On File, Inc.
132 West 31st Street
New York NY 10001

Library of Congress Cataloging-in-Publication Data
Careers in focus. Geriatric care.—2nd ed.
    p. cm.
    Includes index.
    ISBN 0-8160-5866-0 (HC : alk. paper)
    1. Geriatrics—Vocational guidance. I. Title: Geriatric care.
II. J.G. Ferguson Publishing Company.
    RC952.5.C34 2005
    618.97'0231—dc22   2004061991

Ferguson books are available at special discounts when purchased in bulk quantities for businesses, associations, institutions, or sales promotions. Please call our Special Sales Department in New York at (212) 967-8800 or (800) 322-8755.

You can find Ferguson on the World Wide Web at http://www.fergpubco.com

Text design by David Strelecky

Printed in the United States of America

MP JT 10 9 8 7 6 5 4 3 2 1

This book is printed on acid-free paper.

Table of Contents

Introduction

The term *geriatric care* refers to a career field in which professionals work with elderly people. In some cases, these professionals (such as adult day care coordinators and geriatric care managers) have jobs that allow them to focus on providing services solely to elderly clients. In other cases geriatric care professionals (such as creative arts therapists and financial planners) have jobs that allow them to work with a variety of clients, and they may choose to work with or simply find that a large number of their clients are senior citizens.

When you are 15 or 16 years old, age 26 might sound unbearably old to you. When you are 30, age 50 might seem "elderly." So when does "old" officially begin? For the purposes of this book, we use age terms in the same way the federal government does. That is, broad terms such as *elderly, geriatric,* and *senior citizen* refer to a large and diverse group of people age 65 and older.

Geriatric-care careers will be of particular importance in the coming years. One reason for this is that the senior population is large and growing every year. The U.S. Census Bureau reported that approximately 35 million Americans were age 65 or older in 2000, and it expects this population to grow dramatically as people continue to live longer. In 2011, the first members of the large "baby boom" generation (those born from approximately the mid-1940s to the mid-1960s) will begin turning age 65. And a large population with similar interests, concerns, and needs means (among other things) a large consumer group with similar needs and wants. These include specialized medical care, help for daily living activities, and specialized support for dealing with and planning for emotional and end-of-life issues. These resources people turn to for such services are in the hands of professionals such as senior care pharmacists, geriatric social workers, and home health care and hospice nurses.

And that's where you come in. Do you want to provide a service that's in demand by a large number of clients? Do you like the idea of working to make society better? Do the special needs of older people interest you? If your answer to any of these questions is yes, or even maybe, this is the book for you. Although space limitations do not allow us to cover every geriatric care occupation in this book, the careers covered here will give you an idea of the variety of opportunities available in this field.

Each article in *Careers in Focus: Geriatric Care* discusses a particular occupation in detail. The articles appear in Ferguson's

Encyclopedia of Careers and Vocational Guidance. Since the last edition of this book, each article has been updated and revised with the latest information from the U.S. Department of Labor and other sources. Each article is broken down in the following manner.

The **Quick Facts** section provides a brief summary of the career including recommended school subjects, personal skills, work environment, minimum educational requirements, salary ranges, certification or licensing requirements, and employment outlook. This section also provides acronyms and identification numbers for the following government classification indexes: the *Dictionary of Occupational Titles* (DOT), the *Guide for Occupational Exploration* (GOE), the National Occupational Classification (NOC) index, and the Occupational Information Network (O*NET)-Standard Occupational Classification System (SOC) index. The DOT, GOE, and O*NET-SOC indexes have been created by the U.S. government; the NOC index is Canada's career classification system. Readers can use the identification numbers listed in the Quick Facts section to access further information on a career. Print editions of the DOT (*Dictionary of Occupational Titles.* Indianapolis, Ind.: JIST Works, 1991) and GOE (*The Complete Guide for Occupational Exploration.* Indianapolis, Ind.: JIST Works, 1993) are available at libraries, and electronic versions of the NOC (http://www23.hrdc-drhc.gc.ca/2001/e/generic/welcome.shtml) and O*NET-SOC (http://online.onetcenter.org) are available on the World Wide Web. When no DOT, GOE, NOC, or O*NET-SOC numbers are present, this means that the U.S. Department of Labor or the Human Resources Development Canada have not created a numerical designation for this career. In this instance, you will see the acronym "N/A," or not available.

The **Overview** section is a brief introductory description of the duties and responsibilities of someone in the career. Oftentimes, a career may have a variety of job titles. When this is the case, alternative career titles are presented in this section.

The **History** section describes the history of the particular career as it relates to the overall development of its industry or field.

The **Job** describes the primary and secondary duties of the career.

Requirements discusses high school and postsecondary education and training requirements, any certification or licensing necessary, and any other personal requirements for success in the career.

Exploring offers suggestions on how to gain some experience in or knowledge of the particular job before making a firm educational and financial commitment. The focus is on what can be done while still in high school (or in the early years of college) to gain a better understanding of the career.

The **Employers** section gives an overview of typical places of employment for the job.

Starting Out discusses the best ways to land that first job, be it through the college placement office, newspaper ads, or personal contact.

The **Advancement** section describes what kind of career path to expect from the career and how to get on it.

Earnings lists salary ranges and describes the typical fringe benefits.

The **Work Environment** section describes the typical surroundings and conditions of employment—whether indoors or outdoors, noisy or quiet, social or independent, and so on. Also discussed are typical hours worked, any seasonal fluctuations, and the stresses and strains of the job.

The **Outlook** section summarizes the career in terms of the general economy and industry projections. For the most part, Outlook information is obtained from the Bureau of Labor Statistics and is supplemented by information taken from professional associations. Job growth terms follow those used in the *Occupational Outlook Handbook*. Growth described as "much faster than the average" means an increase of 36 percent or more. Growth described as "faster than the average" means an increase of 21–35 percent. Growth described as "about as fast as the average" means an increase of 10–20 percent. Growth described as "more slowly than the average" means an increase of 3–9 percent. Growth described as "little or no change" means an increase of 0–2 percent. "Decline" means a decrease of 1 percent or more.

Each article ends with **For More Information,** which lists organizations that can provide career information on training, education, internships, scholarships, and job placement.

Throughout the book you will also find illustrative photographs of some careers, informative sidebars, and interviews with professionals working in the geriatric care field.

As you explore the wide variety of geriatric care careers that are presented in this book, consider which of them might best suit your personality, strengths, and general career goals. Be sure to contact the organizations listed at the end of each article for more information.

Adult Day Care Coordinators

OVERVIEW

Adult day care coordinators, also called *adult day services coordinators,* direct day service programs for adults who have physical or mental impairments or both. Clients of these programs are usually the elderly, although younger people with impairments, such as those recovering from strokes, may also participate in these programs. Coordinators oversee staff members who provide care, meals, and social activities to day care clients, and they serve as liaisons between their centers and their clients' families.

HISTORY

Adult day care had its beginnings in the 1940s in psychiatric hospitals. It started as an effort to help patients who had been released from mental institutions. Over the next 20 years the focus gradually shifted from psychiatric care to other kinds of health maintenance. The landmark publication *Developing Day Care for Older People,* published by the National Council on the Aging (NCOA) in 1972, provided technical assistance for establishing adult day care; by 1978 there were nearly 300 adult day care centers throughout the United States.

In the 1980s, the first Congressional hearing was held on adult day care programs and the Economic Recovery Act was passed, allowing a tax credit to families with elderly members in day care. NCOA established voluntary standards.

According to the National Adult Day Services Association, more than 3,500 adult day centers are currently operating in the United

States. Approximately 78 percent operate on a nonprofit or public basis, and many are affiliated with larger organizations such as home care, skilled nursing facilities, medical centers, or multipurpose senior organizations.

THE JOB

Adult day care coordinators direct adult day care centers. Although specific duties vary depending on the size of the center and the services it offers, the general responsibility of coordinators is to ensure that their centers provide the necessary care for clients. Such care may include attention to personal hygiene and providing meals, medications, therapies, and social activities.

Although coordinators working in small day care centers may actually perform some services for clients, this is not the norm. Instead, coordinators usually oversee various staff members who provide the caregiving. A large center, for example, might have a nurse, physical therapist, social worker, cook, and several aides. Coordinators are responsible for staff hiring, training, and scheduling. They may meet with staff members either one-on-one or in group sessions to review and discuss plans for the clients.

Overseeing meal planning and preparation is also the responsibility of the adult day services coordinator. In most centers, clients are given a midday meal and usually juices and snacks in the morning and afternoon. Coordinators work with a cook or dietitian to develop well-rounded menus that take into account the nutritional needs of the clients, including any particular restrictions such as diabetic or low-sodium diets. The coordinator may also oversee purchasing and taking inventory of the center's food supply.

The coordinator schedules daily and weekly activities for the day care clients. Depending on the particular needs and abilities of the clients, a recreational schedule might include crafts, games, exercises, reading time, or movies. In some centers, clients are taken on outings to shopping centers, parks, or restaurants. The coordinator plans such outings, arranging for transportation and any reservations or special accommodations that may be necessary. Finally, the coordinator also organizes parties for special events, such as holidays and birthdays.

Finding new activities and visitors for the center is also part of the job. Coordinators might recruit volunteers to teach crafts or music to the clients. Often, church or civic groups come to such facilities to visit with clients. Some such groups institute buddy programs, in which each group member pairs with a day care client to develop an ongoing relationship. The day care coordinator must authorize and monitor any group visits, activities, or programs.

In addition to planning and overseeing the activities of the center and its clients, the adult day care coordinator also works closely with client family members to make sure that each individual is receiving care that best fits his or her needs. This relationship with the client's family usually begins before the client is placed in the day care center.

When a family is considering placing an elderly relative in day care, they often have many questions about the center and its activities. The coordinator meets with family members to show them the center and explain to them how it is run. The coordinator also gathers information about the potential client, including names and phone numbers of doctors and people to contact in case of emergency, lists of medications taken with instructions on when and how they should be administered, and information on allergies, food choices, and daily habits and routines.

After the client is placed in the center, the coordinator may meet periodically with the client's family to update them on how the client is responding to the day care setting. If necessary, the coordinator may advise the family about social services, such as home health care, and refer them to other providers.

Adult day care coordinators may have other duties, depending on the center and how it is owned and operated. For example, they may be responsible for developing and adhering to a budget for the center. In centers licensed or certified by the state, coordinators may ensure that their centers remain in compliance with the regulations and necessary documentation. They may also be responsible for general bookkeeping, bill payment, and office management.

In addition to supervising centers, coordinators may also promote and advertise to the community. They may help with fund-raising, prepare press releases, and speak to various service clubs.

REQUIREMENTS

High School

Because this is a relatively new and growing field, there are no national standards to follow for becoming an adult day care coordinator. Some people have learned their skills on the job; others have taken courses in home nursing or health care; still others have completed bachelor's degrees in areas such as health and human services. As the need for and popularity of day care services continue to grow, more employers will begin to expect coordinators to have at least some formal education. While you are in high school, therefore, you should take classes that prepare you for postsecondary training. These include mathematics, business, family and consumer science classes as well as science classes, such as biology. To improve your understanding of people, take history, psychology, and sociology classes. Because communication is an important skill, English and speech classes are also good choices.

Postsecondary Training

Many employers prefer to hire candidates who meet the standards set by the National Adult Day Services Association (NADSA). In order to meet these standards, a coordinator must have a bachelor's degree in health or social services or a related field, with one year's supervisory experience in a social or health services setting. In preparation for such a career, a college student might choose occupational, recreational, or rehabilitation therapy, or social work or human development. An increasingly popular major for potential adult day care coordinators is gerontology, or geriatrics.

The Association for Gerontology in Higher Education publishes the *Directory of Educational Programs in Gerontology and Geriatrics,* which contains information on more than 750 programs available from the associate's to the post-doctorate level. Although specific courses vary from school to school, most programs consist of classes in social gerontology, biology and physiology of aging, psychology of aging, and sociology of aging. In addition to these four core classes, most programs offer elective courses in such areas as social policy, community services, nutrition and exercise, diversity in aging, health issues, death and dying, and ethics and life extension.

A practicum or field placement is also a part of most gerontology programs. This allows students to obtain experience working with both well-functioning elderly people and those with age-related disabilities.

Certification or Licensing

According to NADSA, there are currently no national standards regarding the qualifications for adult day services workers. NADSA does offer voluntary certification to program assistants. The National Certification Council for Activity Professionals also offers certification to qualified adult day care coordinators. Those who meet the professional standards earn the designation certified activity professional (CAP). See the end of the article for contact information.

Regulations can vary by state. In some states, for example, the agency that a coordinator works for must be licensed or certified by the state health department. Any adult day care center that receives payment from Medicare or from other government agencies must be certified by the state department of health. In these cases, licensing requirements may include requirements for coordinators and other staff members. The trend is toward stricter standards.

Other Requirements

Regardless of what level of education a prospective coordinator has, there are certain personal characteristics that are necessary for success in this field. Compassion and an affinity for the elderly and disabled are vital, as are patience and the desire to help others. You should also be organized and able to manage other workers effectively. Communication skills are very important since you will be working with staff, clients, regulatory agencies, and clients' families.

EXPLORING

There are several ways you can learn more about the career of adult day care coordinator. The first and easiest way is to check your local library for books or articles on aging in order to learn more about the elderly, their issues, and the services available to them. Next, visit a nursing home or adult day care center in order to experience

Things to Consider

The following are just some of questions that families consider when selecting an adult day care center for a loved one:

- Is the environment safe and secure?

- Are there regular social activities?

- Are various therapies (physical, creative arts, occupational) and health monitoring (blood pressure, weight, food/liquid intake) available?

- Does the staff pay attention to and help clients with personal hygiene?

- Will the staff cater to a special diet?

- How many staff members are there per client?

Source: National Adult Day Services Association, http://www.nadsa.org

firsthand what it is like to spend time with and interact with elderly people. Arrange to talk with staff members and the center's coordinator to find out what their day-to-day jobs are like. Your high school guidance counselor may also be able to arrange for a coordinator to give a career talk at your school. Finally, get a volunteer position or part-time job in such a facility. This would allow you to gauge your aptitude for a career in adult day care work.

EMPLOYERS

Adult day care coordinators work at adult day care centers. These may be small or large. It is estimated that there are more than 3,500 adult day care centers currently operating in the United States. Most of them are operated on a nonprofit or public basis, and many are affiliated with large organizations such as nursing homes, hospitals, or multipurpose senior organizations. Standards and work environments vary.

STARTING OUT

In looking for a position as an adult day care coordinator, candidates should first locate and contact all such programs in the area. Checking the local Yellow Pages under Nursing Homes, Residential Care Facilities, Aging Services, or Senior Citizens Services should provide a list of leads. The job seeker might either send a resume and cover letter or call these potential employers directly. Prospective coordinators should also watch for job openings listed in area newspapers and on organizations' websites.

Another means of finding job leads is to become affiliated with a professional association, such as the American Geriatrics Society, the American Association of Homes and Services for the Aging, the Gerontological Society of America, or the National Council on the Aging. Many such organizations have monthly or quarterly newsletters that list job opportunities. Some may even have job banks or referral services.

Job seekers who have received associate's or bachelor's degrees should also check with the career placement offices at their colleges or universities.

ADVANCEMENT

Because the field of aging-related services continues to grow, the potential for advancement for adult day care coordinators is good.

Some coordinators advance by transferring to a larger center that pays better wages. Others eventually start their own centers. Still others advance by moving into management positions in other, similar social service organizations, such as nursing homes, hospices, or government agencies on aging.

An adult day care coordinator might choose to return to school and complete a higher degree, often a master's degree in social work. For those who choose this option, there are many career opportunities in the field of social services. *Social workers*, for example, work with individuals and families dealing with AIDS, cancer, or other debilitating illnesses. They also work for agencies offering various types of counseling, rehabilitation, or crisis intervention.

EARNINGS

Starting salaries for this position depend partly on the experience and education of the coordinator and partly upon the size and location of the day care center. Larger centers located in metropolitan areas tend to offer the highest wages.

According to the Association for Gerontology in Higher Education, beginning annual salaries range from $18,000 to $31,000 for persons with a bachelor's degree and little experience. Generally, coordinators who do not have a bachelor's degree can expect to earn somewhat less. Experienced coordinators with a bachelor's degree employed in large, well-funded centers may earn from $20,000 to $45,000 annually.

In addition to salary, some coordinators are also offered a benefits package, which typically includes health insurance, paid vacation and sick days, and a retirement plan.

WORK ENVIRONMENT

Most adult day care centers have a schedule that corresponds to standard business hours. Most coordinators work a 40-hour week, Monday through Friday, with weekends off.

The coordinator's work environment will vary depending on the size and type of center he or she supervises. Some centers are fairly institutional, resembling children's day care centers or nursing homes. Others have a more residential feel, being carpeted and furnished like a private home. Regardless of the furnishings, the center is typically clean, well lit, and equipped with ramps, rails, and other devices that ensure the safety of clients.

Part of the coordinator's day may be spent in the center's common areas with clients and staff. He or she may also spend time working in an on-site office. If the staff members take clients on outings, the coordinator may accompany them.

Coordinators are on their feet much of the time, ensuring that meals and activities run smoothly and helping staff members when necessary. Attire for the job varies from center to center, ranging from very casual to standard office wear. Most coordinators, however, wear clothing that is comfortable and allows them freedom of movement.

Regardless of the size of the center, coordinators spend the majority of their time working with people, both staff members and day care clients. Working with clients is often very trying. Many of them may have had a stroke or have Alzheimer's disease, and they may be confused, uncooperative, or even hostile. The job may also be emotionally taxing for the coordinator who becomes attached to his or her clients. Most adults who use a day care center are elderly or permanently disabled; for this reason, day care staff must frequently deal with the decline and eventual death of their clients.

OUTLOOK

The outlook for all human services workers, and adult day care coordinators in particular, is expected to be excellent through 2012, growing at a rate that is much faster than the average. The main reason for this is that the senior citizen population is growing rapidly. According to a study conducted by the Department of Health and Human Services, by 2030 there will be 70 million older persons in the United States, which is almost twice the number that existed in 2000. Coupled with this growing elderly population will be a decreasing number of caregivers because of increased divorce rates, smaller families, delayed childbearing trends, and more men and women in the workforce. Given these projections, adult day care will be used more frequently as a cost-efficient and preferable alternative to nursing homes.

FOR MORE INFORMATION

For information on aging and services for the elderly, contact
American Association of Homes and Services for the Aging
2519 Connecticut Avenue, NW
Washington, DC 20008-1520
Tel: 202-783-2242
http://www.aahsa.org

AGHE, a section of the Gerontological Society of America, promotes education in the field of aging and offers a directory of gerontology and geriatrics programs. Visit the website, http://www.careersinaging. com, to read Careers in Aging: Consider the Opportunities.

Association for Gerontology in Higher Education (AGHE)
1030 15th Street, NW, Suite 240
Washington, DC 20005-1503
Tel: 202-289-9806
Email: aghetemp@aghe.org
http://www.aghe.org

For career information and student resources, contact
Gerontological Society of America
1030 15th Street, NW, Suite 250
Washington, DC 20005
Tel: 202-842-1275
Email: geron@geron.org
http://www.geron.org

For information on the history of adult day service and day service facts, contact
National Adult Day Services Association
722 Grant Street, Suite L
Herndon, VA 20170
Tel: 800-558-5301
Email: info@nadsa.org
http://www.nadsa.org

This organization can provide information on services, including adult day care, available across the country.
National Association of Area Agencies on Aging
1730 Rhode Island Avenue, NW, Suite 1200
Washington, DC 20036
Tel: 202-872-0888
http://www.n4a.org

For information on certification, contact
National Certification Council for Activity Professionals
PO Box 62589
Virginia Beach, VA 23466
Tel: 757-552-0653
http://www.nccap.org

To learn about developments and current issues in the aging field, visit the following website.

National Council on the Aging
300 D Street, SW, Suite 801
Washington, DC 20024
Tel: 202-479-1200
http://www.ncoa.org

Creative Arts Therapists

QUICK FACTS

School Subjects
Art
Music
Theater/dance

Personal Skills
Artistic
Helping/teaching

Work Environment
Primarily indoors
Primarily one location

Minimum Education Level
Master's degree

Salary Range
$15,000 to $35,000 to
$81,000

Certification or Licensing
Required by all states

Outlook
About as fast as the average

DOT
076

GOE
10.02.02

NOC
3144

O*NET-SOC
N/A

OVERVIEW

Creative arts therapists treat and rehabilitate people with mental, physical, and emotional disabilities. They use the creative processes of music, art, dance/movement, drama, psychodrama, and poetry in their therapy sessions to determine the underlying causes of problems and to help patients achieve therapeutic goals. Creative arts therapists usually specialize in one particular type of therapeutic activity. The specific objectives of the therapeutic activities vary according to the needs of the patient and the setting of the therapy program.

HISTORY

Creative arts therapy programs are fairly recent additions to the health care field. Although many theories of mental and physical therapy have existed for centuries, it has been only in the last 70 years or so that health care professionals have truly realized the healing powers of music, art, dance, and other forms of artistic self-expression.

Art therapy is based on the idea that people who can't discuss their problems with words must have another outlet for self-expression. In the early 1900s, psychiatrists began to look more closely at their patients' artwork, realizing that there could be links between the emotional or psychological illness and the art. Sigmund Freud even did some preliminary research into the artistic expression of his patients.

In the 1930s, art educators discovered that children often expressed their thoughts better with pictures and role-playing than they did through verbalization. Children often don't know the words they need to explain how they feel or how to make their needs known to adults. Researchers began to look into art as a way to treat children who were traumatized by abuse, neglect, illness, or other physical or emotional disabilities.

During and after World War II, the Department of Veterans Affairs (VA) developed and organized various art, music, and dance activities for patients in VA hospitals. These activities had a dramatic effect on the physical and mental well-being of the World War II veterans, and creative arts therapists began to help treat and rehabilitate patients in other health care settings.

Because of early breakthroughs with children and veterans, the number of arts therapists has increased greatly over the past few decades, and the field has expanded to include drama, psychodrama, and poetry, in addition to the original areas of music, art, and dance. Today, creative arts therapists work with diverse populations of patients in a wide range of facilities, and they focus on the specific needs of a vast spectrum of disorders and disabilities. Colleges and universities offer degree programs in many types of therapies, and national associations for registering and certifying creative arts therapists work to monitor training programs and to ensure the professional integrity of the therapists working in the various fields.

THE JOB

Creative arts therapy taps into the subconscious and gives people a mode of expression in an uncensored environment. This is important because before patients can begin to heal, they must first identify their feelings. Once they recognize their feelings, they can begin to develop an understanding of the relationship between their feelings and their behavior.

The main goal of a creative arts therapist is to improve the client's physical, mental, and emotional health. Before therapists begin any treatment, they meet with a team of other health care professionals. After determining the strength, limitations, and interests of their client, they create a program to promote positive change and growth. The creative arts therapist continues to confer with the other health care workers as the program progresses, and alters the program according to the client's progress. How these goals are reached depends on the unique specialty of the therapist in question.

"It's like sitting in the woods waiting for a fawn to come out." That is how Barbara Fish, former Director of Activity Therapy for the Illinois Department of Mental Health and Developmental Disabilities,

Chicago Metropolitan and Adolescent Services, describes her experience as she waits patiently for a sexually abused patient to begin to trust her. The patient is extraordinarily frightened because of the traumatic abuse she has suffered. This may be the first time in the patient's life that she is in an environment of acceptance and support. It may take months or even years before the patient begins to trust the therapist, "come out of the woods," and begin to heal.

In some cases, especially when the clients are adolescents, they may have become so detached from their feelings that they can physically act out without consciously knowing the reasons for their behavior. This detachment from their emotions creates a great deal of psychological pain. With the help of a creative arts therapist, clients can begin to communicate their subconscious feelings both verbally and nonverbally. They can express their emotions in a variety of ways without having to name them.

Creative arts therapists work with all age groups: young children, adolescents, adults, and senior citizens. They can work in individual, group, or family sessions. The approach of the therapist, however, depends on the specific needs of the client or group. For example, if an individual is feeling overwhelmed by too many options or stimuli, the therapist may give him or her only a plain piece of paper and a pencil to work with that day.

Fish has three ground rules for her art therapy sessions with disturbed adolescents: respect yourself, respect other people, and respect property. The therapy groups are limited to five patients per group. She begins the session by asking each person in the group how he or she is feeling that day. By carefully listening to their responses, a theme may emerge that will determine the direction of the therapy. For example, if anger is reoccurring in their statements, Fish may ask them to draw a line down the center of a piece of paper. On one side, she will ask them to draw how anger looks and, on the other side, how feeling sad looks. Then, once the drawing is complete, she will ask them to compare the two pictures and see that their anger may be masking their feelings of sadness, loneliness, and disappointment. As patients begin to recognize their true feelings, they develop better control of their behavior.

To reach their patients, creative arts therapists can use a variety of mediums, including visual art, music, dance, drama, or poetry or other kinds of creative writing. Creative arts therapists usually specialize in a specific medium, becoming a music therapist, drama therapist, dance therapist, art therapist, or poetry therapist. "In my groups we use poetry and creative writing," Fish explains. "We do all kinds of things to get at what is going on at an unconscious level."

Music therapists use musical lessons and activities to improve a patient's self-confidence and self-awareness, to relieve states of depression, and to improve physical dexterity. For example, a music therapist treating a patient with Alzheimer's might play songs from the patient's past in order to stimulate long- and short-term memory, soothe feelings of agitation, and increase a sense of reality.

Art therapists use art in much the same manner. The art therapist may encourage and teach patients to express their thoughts, feelings, and anxieties via sketching, drawing, painting, or sculpting. Art therapy is especially helpful in revealing patterns of domestic abuse in families. Children involved in such a situation may depict scenes of family life with violent details or portray a certain family member as especially frightening or threatening.

Dance/movement therapists develop and conduct dance/movement sessions to help improve the physical, mental, and emotional health of their patients. Dance and movement therapy is also used as a way of assessing a patient's progress toward reaching therapeutic goals.

There are other types of creative arts therapists as well. *Drama therapists* use role-playing, pantomime (the telling of a story by the use of expressive body or facial movements), puppetry, improvisation, and original scripted dramatization to evaluate and treat patients. *Poetry therapists* and *bibliotherapists* use the written and spoken word to treat patients.

REQUIREMENTS
High School
To become a creative arts therapist, you will need a bachelor's degree, so take a college preparatory curriculum while in high school. You should become as proficient as possible with the methods and tools related to the type of creative arts therapy you wish to pursue. When therapists work with patients they must be able to concentrate completely on the patient rather than on learning how to use tools or techniques. For example, if you want to become involved in music therapy, you need to be familiar with musical instruments as well as music theory. A good starting point for a music therapist is to study piano or guitar.

In addition to courses such as drama, art, music, and English, you should consider taking an introductory class in psychology. Also, a communication class will give you an understanding of the various ways people communicate, both verbally and nonverbally.

Postsecondary Training

To become a creative arts therapist you must earn at least a bachelor's degree, usually in the area in which you wish to specialize. For example, those studying to be art therapists typically have undergraduate degrees in studio art, art education, or psychology with a strong emphasis on art courses as well.

In most cases, however, you will also need a graduate degree before you can gain certification as a professional or advance in your chosen field. Requirements for admission to graduate schools vary by program, so you would be wise to contact the graduate programs you are interested in to find out about their admissions policies. For some fields you may be required to submit a portfolio of your work along with the written application. Professional organizations can be a good source of information regarding high-quality programs. For example, both the American Art Therapy Association and the American Music Therapy Association provide lists of schools that meet their standards for approval. (Contact information for both associations are listed at the end of this article.)

In graduate school, your study of psychology and the arts field you are interested in will be in-depth. Classes for someone seeking a master's in art therapy, for example, may include group psychotherapy, foundation of creativity theory, assessment and treatment planning, and art therapy presentation. In addition to classroom study you will also complete an internship or supervised practicum (that is, work with clients). Depending on your program, you may also need to write a thesis or present a final artistic project before receiving your degree.

Certification or Licensing

Typically, the nationally recognized association or certification board specific to your field of choice offers registration and certification. For example, the Art Therapy Credentials Board (ATCB) offers registration and certification to art therapists, and the American Dance Therapy Association offers registration to dance therapists. In general, requirements for registration include completing an approved therapy program and having a certain amount of experience working with clients. Requirements for higher levels of registration or certification generally involve having additional work experience and passing a written exam.

For a specific example, consider the certification process for an art therapist: an art therapist may receive the designation art therapist registered (ART) from the ATCB after completing a graduate program and having some experience working with clients. The next level, then, is to become an art therapist registered-board certified

(ART-BC) by passing a written exam. To retain certification status, therapists must complete a certain amount of continuing education.

Many registered creative arts therapists also hold additional licenses in other fields, such as social work, education, mental health, or marriage and family therapy. In some states, creative arts therapists need licensing depending on their place of work. For specific information on licensing in your field, you will need to check with your state's licensing board. Creative arts therapists are also often members of other professional associations, including the American Psychological Association, the American Association of Marriage and Family Therapists, and the American Counseling Association.

Other Requirements

To succeed in this line of work, you should have a strong desire to help others seek positive change in their lives. All types of creative arts therapists must be able to work well with other people—both patients and other health professionals—in the development and implementation of therapy programs. You must have the patience and the stamina to teach and practice therapy with patients for whom progress is often very slow because of their various physical and emotional disorders. A therapist must always keep in mind that even a tiny amount of progress might be extremely significant for some patients and their families. A good sense of humor is also a valuable trait.

EXPLORING

There are many ways to explore the possibility of a career as a creative arts therapist. Write to professional associations for information on therapy careers. Talk with people working in the creative arts therapy field and perhaps arrange to observe a creative arts therapy session. Look for part-time or summer jobs or volunteer at a hospital, clinic, nursing home, or any of a number of health care facilities.

A summer job as an aide at a camp for disabled children, for example, may help provide insight into the nature of creative arts therapy, including both its rewards and demands. Such experience can be very valuable in deciding if you are suited to the inherent frustrations of a therapy career.

EMPLOYERS

Creative arts therapists usually work as members of an interdisciplinary health care team that may include physicians, nurses, social workers, psychiatrists, and psychologists. Although often employed in hospitals,

Words to Know

acting out: uncontrolled, usually aggressive behavior in which a patient responds to emotionally stressful experiences

creativity coach: person hired by a company or individual to help nurture the creative process

impulsive disorder: any disorder in which a person acts primarily on impulse without considering the consequences of the action

portfolio: collection of artwork used to provide examples of an artist's skills and techniques

therapists also work in rehabilitation centers, nursing homes, day treatment facilities, shelters for battered women, pain and stress management clinics, substance abuse programs, hospices, and correctional facilities. Others maintain their own private practices. Many creative arts therapists work with children in grammar and high schools, either as therapists or art teachers. Some arts therapists teach or conduct research in the creative arts at colleges and universities.

STARTING OUT

After earning a bachelor's degree in a particular field, you should complete your certification, which may include an internship or assistantship. Unpaid training internships often can lead to a first job in the field. Graduates can use the placement office at their college or university to help them find positions in the creative arts therapy field. Many professional associations also compile lists of job openings to assist their members.

Creative arts therapists who are new to the field might consider doing volunteer work at a nonprofit community organization, correctional facility, or neighborhood association to gain some practical experience. Therapists who want to start their own practice can host group therapy sessions in their homes. Creative arts therapists may also wish to associate with other members of the alternative health care field in order to gain experience and build a client base.

ADVANCEMENT

With more experience, therapists can move into supervisory, administrative, and teaching positions. Often, the supervision of interns can resemble a therapy session. The interns will discuss their feelings and ask questions they may have regarding their work with clients. How did they handle their clients? What were the reactions to what their clients said or did? What could they be doing to help more? The supervising therapist helps the interns become competent creative arts therapists.

Many therapists have represented the profession internationally. Barbara Fish was invited to present her paper "Art Therapy with Children and Adolescents" at the University of Helsinki. Additionally, Fish spoke in Finland at a three-day workshop exploring the use and effectiveness of arts therapy with children and adolescents. Raising the public and professional awareness of creative arts therapy is an important concern for many therapists.

EARNINGS

A therapist's annual salary depends on experience, level of training, and education. Working on a hospital staff or being self-employed also affects annual income. According to the American Art Therapy Association (AATA), entry-level art therapists earn annual salaries of approximately $25,000. Median annual salaries range from $28,000 to $38,000, and AATA reports that top earnings for salaried administrators ranged from $40,000 and $60,000 annually. Those who have Ph.D.'s and are licensed for private practice can earn between $75 and $90 per hour, according to AATA; however, professional expenses such as insurance and office rental must be paid by those in private practice.

The American Music Therapy Association reported average annual salaries for music therapists as $34,893 in 2000. Salaries varied from that average by region, most by less than $2,000 a year, with the highest average salaries reported in the New England states at $41,600. Salaries reported by its members ranged from $15,000 to $81,000. The average annual earnings for music therapists with more than 20 years of professional experience was $43,306 in 2000.

The annual salary for therapists working for the government is determined by the agency they work for, their level of education and experience, and their responsibilities. An August 2002 job posting by the Delaware Department of Health & Social Services, for example, advertised an opening for a certified creative arts therapist that offered the salary range of $26,094 to $32,618, based on the applicant's qualifications.

Benefits depend on the employer but generally include paid vacation time, health insurance, and paid sick days. Those who are in private practice must provide their own benefits.

WORK ENVIRONMENT

Most creative arts therapists work a typical 40-hour, five-day workweek; at times, however, they may have to work extra hours. The number of patients under a therapist's care depends on the specific employment setting. Although many therapists work in hospitals, they may also be employed in such facilities as clinics, rehabilitation centers, children's homes, schools, and nursing homes. Some therapists maintain service contracts with several facilities. For instance, a therapist might work two days a week at a hospital, one day at a nursing home, and the rest of the week at a rehabilitation center.

Most buildings are pleasant, comfortable, and clean places in which to work. Experienced creative arts therapists might choose to be self-employed, working with patients in their own studios. In such a case, the therapist might work more irregular hours to accommodate patient schedules. Other therapists might maintain a combination of service contract work with one or more facilities in addition to a private caseload of clients referred to them by other health care professionals. Whether therapists work on service contracts with various facilities or maintain private practices, they must deal with all of the business and administrative details and worries that go along with being self-employed.

OUTLOOK

The American Art Therapy Association notes that this is a growing field. Demand for new therapists is created as medical professionals and the general public become aware of the benefits gained through art therapies. Although enrollment in college therapy programs is increasing, new graduates are usually able to find jobs. In cases where an individual is unable to find a full-time position, a therapist might obtain service contracts for part-time work at several facilities.

Job openings in facilities such as nursing homes should continue to increase as the elderly population grows over the next few decades. Advances in medical technology and the recent practice of early discharge from hospitals should also create new opportunities in managed care facilities, chronic pain clinics, and cancer care facilities. The demand for therapists of all types should continue to increase as more people become aware of the need to help disabled patients in creative ways. Some drama therapists and psychodramatists are also finding employment opportunities outside of the usual health care field. Such therapists might conduct therapy sessions at corporate sites to enhance the personal effectiveness and growth of employees.

FOR MORE INFORMATION

For more detailed information about your field of interest, contact the following organizations:

American Art Therapy Association
1202 Allanson Road
Mundelein, IL 60060-3808
Tel: 888-290-0878
Email: info@arttherapy.org
http://www.arttherapy.org

American Dance Therapy Association
2000 Century Plaza, Suite 108
10632 Little Patuxent Parkway
Columbia, MD 21044
Tel: 410-997-4040
Email: info@adta.org
http://www.adta.org

American Music Therapy Association
8455 Colesville Road, Suite 1000
Silver Spring, MD 20910
Tel: 301-589-3300
Email: info@musictherapy.org
http://www.musictherapy.org

American Society of Group Psychotherapy and Psychodrama
301 North Harrison Street, Suite 508
Princeton, NJ 08540
Tel: 609-452-1339
Email: asgpp@asgpp.org
http://www.asgpp.org

National Association for Drama Therapy
15 Post Side Lane
Pittsford, NY 14534
Tel: 585-381-5618
http://www.nadt.org

National Association for Poetry Therapy
16861 SW 6th Street
Pembroke Pines, FL 33027
Tel: 866-844-NAPT
http://www.poetrytherapy.org

For an overview of the various types of art therapy, visit the NCATA website.

National Coalition of Arts Therapies Associations (NCATA)
c/o AMTA
8455 Colesville Road, Suite 1000
Silver Spring, MD 20910
Tel: 301-224-9146
http://www.nccata.org

Elder Law Attorneys

OVERVIEW

Lawyers, or *attorneys,* work in our legal system as advocates and advisers. As advocates, they represent the rights of their clients in trials and depositions or in front of administrative and government bodies. As advisers, attorneys counsel clients on how the law affects business or personal decisions, such as the purchase of property or the creation of a will. Lawyers can represent individuals, businesses, and corporations. *Elder law attorneys* are lawyers who specialize in providing legal services for the elderly and, in some cases, the disabled. Unlike other lawyers who deal with one field of law, such as tax lawyers, elder law attorneys often deal with several fields of law when providing services to their clients. Some of the most common elder law issues include guardianship or conservatorship, public benefits (Medicaid, Medicare, and Social Security), probate and estate planning, health and long-term care planning, and elder abuse cases. The National Academy of Elder Law Attorneys Inc. (NAELA) reports that its current membership is more than 3,000. In addition, there are thousands of attorneys who practice elder law as a part of a law practice that encompasses a range of other areas.

HISTORY

Over the centuries, societies have built up systems of law that have been studied and drawn upon by later governments. The earliest known law is the Code of Hammurabi, developed about 1800 B.C. by the ruler of the Sumerians. Another early set of laws was the law of Moses, also known as the Ten Commandments. Every set of laws, no matter when it was introduced, has been accompanied by the need for someone to explain those laws and help others live under them.

Much modern European law was organized and refined by legal experts assembled by Napoleon; their body of law was known as the Napoleonic Code. English colonists coming to America brought English common law, which influenced the development of much of American law. As the population in the country grew and the number of businesses increased, those who knew the law were in high demand. The two main kinds of law are civil and criminal, but many other specialty areas are also prevalent today. When the United States was a young nation, most lawyers were general law practitioners; they knew and worked with all the laws for their clients. Today, as laws have grown more complex, an increasing number of lawyers specialize and limit their practices to certain areas, such as tax law, corporate law, and intellectual property law.

In the 20th century, the number of Americans over the age of 65 increased dramatically. One significant reason for this increase was medical and technological advances that extended life spans. As the older population became larger, its members began to experience problems and have concerns that affected all of society, including financing the post-retirement years, the increased need for nursing homes and medical/geriatric care, the legal and ethical issues regarding the care of individuals with diminished capabilities, and the frequent difficulty of getting the appropriate public benefits. Senior citizens who may never have seen an attorney in their lives can find themselves in need of legal advice and advocacy. Out of necessity, elder law has developed to meet their needs. In addition, one of the largest generations in our country's history—the "baby boomers" who were born between 1945 and 1965—will soon become a part of this older generation (approximately from the early 2010s to the 2030s). As this large generation ages, the demand for elder law attorneys should increase.

THE JOB

Lawyers can give legal advice and, when necessary, represent their clients' interests in court. Regardless of their area of expertise, an attorney's job is to help clients know and understand their legal rights and to help them assert those rights before a judge, jury, government agency, or other legal forum, such as an arbitration panel.

Elder law attorneys focus on the needs of their elderly clients, using a variety of legal tools and techniques to meet their goals in an efficient, fiscally responsible, and legally sound manner. Elder law attorneys deal with the whole of the legal needs of their clients. Because of this, their responsibilities are many. They may help one client with estate planning; they may counsel another client about planning for mental incapacity and compose an alternative decision-making document that will allow another family member, for example, to make decisions about that client's health care; and they may assist yet another client in planning for possible long-term care needs, including nursing home care. Locating the appropriate type of care, coordinating private and public resources to finance the cost of care, and working to ensure the client's right to quality care are all part of the elder law practice.

Elder law lawyers must know the law's position on a variety of issues, including health and long-term care planning, surrogate decision-making (that is, when the client has appointed someone, most likely a relative, to make financial or other decisions when the client is unable to), obtaining public benefits (including Medicaid, Medicare, and Social Security), managing diminished capacity (such as when the client can no longer think clearly), and the conservation and administration of the older person's estate (including wills, trusts, and probate). In advising about these matters, elder law attorneys must know about the tax consequences for clients when they decide on a certain action (such as putting money in a trust); attorneys must also recognize when they need to seek out more sophisticated tax information from an expert and do so for the best interests of their clients. In addition, elder law attorneys must be able to recognize cases of abuse, neglect, and exploitation of an older client. An elder law attorney must also be familiar with professional and non-legal resources and services that are publicly and privately available to meet the needs of the older person. Elder law lawyers can then refer clients to these resources, which may include adult day care centers, community transportation, and food services. Elder law encompasses more than just legal planning; it deals with a larger realm of life planning.

In many cases, a crisis is what brings a new client to an elder law attorney. Common situations include middle-income families concerned about paying for a parent's long-term care and nursing home care; families with an older member whose ability to think clearly and live independently is diminishing; older people wanting to ensure their wishes are respected when their health deteriorates; families struggling with retirement and/or assisted-living decisions, contracts, and expenses; and families or seniors faced with issues of age discrimination, exploitation, or abuse.

Elder law attorneys must conduct their practices ethically. They must understand their clients, know which confidences can be shared with which family members, and know when and how to seek other professionals, whether about medical, financial, insurance, or tax issues, to best meet the needs of the clients. The attorney must also recognize situations where a client's wishes clash with those of the family and then determine the best way of handling the issues to best serve the client.

REQUIREMENTS

High School

To become a lawyer you will need to get a college degree and a law degree after you graduate from high school. To start preparing for this later education and career, take a college preparatory curriculum, including math, science, and even a foreign language, while in high school. Be sure to take courses in social studies, government, history, and economics to prepare for law studies. English courses are also important for building your writing, researching, and speaking skills. And because lawyers often use technology to research and interpret the law, take advantage of any computer-related classes or experience you can get. Even surfing the Internet can provide experience in doing research online.

Postsecondary Training

To enter any law school approved by the American Bar Association, you must satisfactorily complete at least three, and usually four, years of college work. Most law schools do not specify any particular courses for prelaw education. The traditional majors for college students intending to pursue a postgraduate law degree are history, English, philosophy, political science, economics, and business. Other successful law students have focused their undergraduate studies in areas as diverse as art, music theory, computer science, engineering, nursing, and education. A college student planning to specialize in elder law might also take courses significantly related to that area, such as social sciences, psychology, economics, and courses related to health care.

To gain admission to law school, most programs require applicants to take the Law School Admission Test (LSAT). The LSAT tests students on analytical thinking, writing, and problem-solving skills. Most full-time law degree programs take three years to complete.

There are currently 185 approved law schools in the United States. State authorities approve additional programs, many of them part-time or night school programs that can be completed in four years. You should contact law schools you are interested in to find out specific requirements for their programs. College guidance counselors and professors may also be valuable sources of information.

The first year of typical law school programs consists of required courses, such as legal writing and research, contracts, criminal law, constitutional law, torts, and property. First-year law students are required to read and study thousands of legal cases. The second and third years are usually focused on specialized courses of interest to the student. In the case of elder law, students might take course work in public policy, health law, medical ethics, and geriatrics.

Upon completing law school, students usually receive the juris doctor (J.D.) degree or bachelor of laws (LL.B.) degree.

Certification or Licensing

To obtain a law license, lawyers (regardless of their specialization) must be admitted to the bar association of the state in which they will practice. Bar admission standards in most states require that students graduate from an approved law school and that they pass a bar examination in the state in which they intend to practice. These exams, usually lasting two days, have questions about various areas of the law, such as constitutional law and criminal law. The tests may also include an essay section and a professional responsibility section. It is important to note, however, that each state sets its own standards for taking the bar exam, and a few states allow exceptions to the educational requirements. For example, a small number of states allow a person who has spent several years reading law in a law office and has some law school experience to take the state bar exam. A few states allow people who have completed law study through correspondence programs to take the bar. In addition, some states require that newly graduated lawyers serve a period of clerkship in an established law firm before they are eligible to take the bar examination. Because of such variations, you will need to contact the bar examiners board of your state for specific information on its requirements.

Specialized voluntary certification is available for elder law attorneys. The National Elder Law Foundation (NELF) offers certification to attorneys who have been in practice five years or longer, have spent at least 16 hours per week (over three years) practicing elder law, have handled at least 60 elder law matters, and have had at least 45 hours of continuing legal education in elder law. After five years, certified attorneys must be recertified to maintain their status.

Other Requirements

All lawyers have to be effective communicators, work well with people, and be able to find creative solutions to problems, such as complex court cases. Elder lawyers, however, need to have some special skills and personality characteristics. They need to understand how aging affects the mind and body, how conflicts can arise among family members regarding the best interests of an elderly member, and how the family's wishes sometimes are in conflict with those of the older person. This work requires perceptiveness, ethics, and diplomacy. Barbara Fox, an attorney practicing elder law at Ray, Fleischer, and Fox in Chicago, asserts that listening to and truly understanding a client is one of the most important skills for an elder law attorney. "People come in with family members who may have differing concerns and opinions, but you need to focus on the wants and needs of your client. It's important always to remember who your client is."

EXPLORING

You can explore this profession by finding out more about being a lawyer and by gaining experience working with the elderly. To learn more about the legal profession in general, sit in on some trials at your local or state courthouse. Watch the lawyers and take note of what they do. Write down questions you have and terms or actions you don't understand so you can research them later. Work with your guidance counselor to set up an informational interview with a lawyer willing to answer questions about the career. You may also be able to "job shadow" this person for part of a workday or more. By doing this, you can see some of the typical daily work of a lawyer. You may even be able to help with some tasks, such as filing.

The Internet is also a good source of information. You can go to law-related sites to learn more about legal terminology, current court cases, and the field of law in general. Some sites that would be particularly beneficial to visit include those of the ABA, NAELA, and NELF. (See the end of this article for the Web addresses.) You can also try to get part-time or summer work in a lawyer's office. You may only be answering phones, filing office papers, or typing letters, but this work will give you excellent exposure to the profession.

It will also be important for you to get experience working with the elderly, either on a paid or a volunteer basis. Contact local nursing homes, senior centers, and volunteer groups providing services, such as Meals on Wheels, to find out what opportunities are avail-

What an Elder Law Attorney Needs to Know

The Board of Certification of the National Elder Law Foundation requires that certified elder law attorneys be knowledgeable in the following subjects:

- Health and long-term care planning

- Public benefits (Medicare, Medicaid, Social Security)

- Surrogate decision making (including powers of attorney and guardianship)

- Older persons legal capacity

- Estate issues, including wills, trusts, and probate of an estate

The Board also expects certified elder law attorneys to be capable of recognizing and handling the issues often involved in counseling and representing older people, such as abuse or neglect, insurance, housing, long-term care, and retirement issues. Elder law attorneys must also be aware of public and private non-legal resources that are available for older persons, and they must know when and how to recommend such services.

For more information, visit http://www.nelf.org.

able. By working with the elderly population, you will start to learn about their specific needs, concerns, and opinions.

EMPLOYERS

The majority of practicing elder law attorneys in the United States work in private practice, either in law firms or alone. While it may seem that the best employment possibilities might be found in large cities and metropolitan areas, there is also fierce competition in these places. Many attorneys practice elder law in addition to other areas of law. Additionally, clients often come to their regular attorneys for elder issues that arise in their lives. Since elder law is so client-oriented, the logical approach is to practice where there is a large population of elderly people; therefore, smaller, more rural areas offer numerous opportunities. In addition, the cost of living is lower in these areas, and since the majority of people seeking elder law attorneys are not wealthy and cannot pay astronomical fees, the elder law attorney will find living on a typical income easier in these areas.

STARTING OUT

After graduation from law school, a lawyer's first task is to pass the state bar examination. A new lawyer will often find a job with a law firm, doing research for other lawyers until passing the bar examination and becoming licensed to practice law. Beginning lawyers usually do not go into solo practice right away. It is difficult to become established, and the experience of working beside established lawyers is helpful to the fledgling lawyer. Newly admitted lawyers typically do research and routine work at first. Specialization usually occurs after a lawyer has some experience in general practice, although lawyers at smaller firms might find themselves guided to particular areas earlier. After a few years of successful experience, a lawyer may be ready to go out on his or her own.

Many new lawyers are recruited directly from law school by law firms or other employers. Recruiters come to the law school and interview possible hires. Recent graduates can also get job leads from local and state bar associations.

To start building a practice in elder law, take as many cases that fall into the realm of elder law as you can and become a member of the NAELA. When you have enough experience under your belt and meet the necessary qualifications, become certified as an elder law attorney with NELF.

ADVANCEMENT

Lawyers with outstanding ability may expect to go a long way in their profession. Beginning lawyers generally start out doing routine research tasks, but as they prove themselves and develop their abilities, opportunities for advancement will arise. They may be promoted to junior partner in a law firm or establish their own practice focused on elder law.

Advancement for elder law attorneys can also take the form of leadership positions in nonprofit organizations that serve to advance education and competence in the field. There are many opportunities to make a contribution to the elderly population by working to support or change the laws and policies that affect senior citizens. In this unique area of legal practice, the potential for reward, although usually not as financially large as other areas of the law, is great.

EARNINGS

Beginning lawyers earn a modest salary, but the potential for higher earnings builds quickly with solid experience. A lawyer just starting out in solo practice may barely make ends meet for the first few years, especially since many law-school graduates carry $70,000–$80,000 in student loan debt.

According to the U.S. Department of Labor, lawyers had a median salary of $90,290 in 2002. The lowest paid 10 percent earned less than $44,490, and the highest paid 10 percent earned more than $145,600.

According to a 2001 survey conducted by the National Association of Law Placement, median salaries for law graduates six months after graduation were $60,000. Graduates working as judges' clerks or in government made median salaries of $40,300, while those working in private practice earned median salaries of $90,000. Although salaries for private practice law are attractive, it is important to remember that lawyers just starting out may barely make ends meet for the first few years. Most law-school graduates carry upwards of $70,000 in student loans. Thus, although many graduates may want to work in public service and government law, many take jobs in private practice in order to gain a stronger financial foothold.

Benefits and bonuses vary widely in this field. Many attorneys are sole practitioners and therefore don't receive company benefits such as paid vacation, health insurance, and retirement plans. Generally, lawyers who are partners in larger firms may enjoy more generous benefits packages and perks than those with a sole practice.

WORK ENVIRONMENT

Lawyers typically enjoy a pleasant, although busy, work environment. Law offices are usually designed to impress clients and can be quite comfortable. Lawyers may also spend significant time in law libraries or record rooms or in the homes and offices of clients. Courtrooms are usually orderly and efficient workplaces. However, many elder law lawyers never work in a courtroom, and, unless directly involved in litigation, they may never work at a trial.

Working hours for most lawyers are usually regular business hours. Many lawyers, however, have to work long hours when a client's case demands it, spending evenings and weekends preparing cases and materials and working with clients. Besides the time spent working directly on a client's needs, lawyers must always keep up with the latest developments in the profession. Lawyers who work in law firms must often work long hours for senior partners in order to advance in the firm. Spending long weekend hours doing research and interviewing people should be expected.

Elder law attorneys, more than other types of lawyers, can expect to put in more hours visiting their clients in their homes or care facilities, since traveling to the attorney's office may be challenging for some clients. Attorneys who specialize in elder law should be prepared for the realities of life for the elderly, as they are likely to be exposed to various types and stages of illness or infirmity and environments that can be disturbing to some.

OUTLOOK

According to the U.S. Department of Labor, the demand for all lawyers is expected to grow as fast as the average through 2012, but those in the specialty of elder law will have the advantage of a rapidly growing elderly population, increasingly complex laws, and unprecedented health care issues. All of these factors combine to make for a substantial client base in need of elder law attorneys. It is estimated that 40 percent of people over 65 will require nursing home or other long-term care at some point, but few of them have planned financially for that eventuality. People are living longer and encountering a variety of health care problems, many of them debilitating. The sheer numbers of elderly people alone point to a promising future in this career.

However, the outlook is also affected by governmental changes and public policy. Barbara Fox points out that since a majority of elder law clients are seeking legal advice and assistance for Medicare/Medicaid issues, the outlook for the profession is significantly affected by changes in law. If there is a decrease in public benefits, this will affect the workload for elder law attorneys. She also advises that many people do not seek out an elder law attorney in particular for issues such as long-range planning, asset protection, guardianship, and probate practices; rather, they are likely to bring these issues to their regular attorney. In other words, attorneys who may not specialize in elder law often handle a large number of cases involving elder law issues.

A record number of law school graduates has created strong competition for jobs, and new attorneys, even those with an eye toward elder law specialization, will initially face stiff competition for jobs.

Lawyers in solo practice will find it hard to earn a living until their practice and reputation are fully established. The best opportunities exist in small towns or suburbs of large cities, where there is less competition and new lawyers can meet potential clients more easily.

FOR MORE INFORMATION

For information about law student services, approved law schools, and the ABA Commission on Legal Problems of the Elderly, contact
American Bar Association (ABA)
Service Center
541 North Fairbanks Court
Chicago, IL 60611
Tel: 800-285-2211
http://www.abanet.org

For information on AALS members, contact
Association of American Law Schools (AALS)
1201 Connecticut Avenue, NW, Suite 800
Washington, DC 20036-2605
Tel: 202-296-8851
Email: aals@aals.org
http://www.aals.org

For information on elder law, contact
National Academy of Elder Law Attorneys Inc.
1604 North Country Club Road
Tucson, AZ 85716
Tel: 520-881-4005
http://www.naela.org

For information about certification in elder law, contact
National Elder Law Foundation
1604 North Country Club Road
Tucson, AZ 85716
Tel: 520-881-1076
http://www.nelf.org

For more information on issues affecting the elderly, contact the following organization:
National Institute on Aging
Building 31, Room 5C27
31 Center Drive, MSC 2292
Bethesda, MD 20892
Tel: 301-496-1752
http://www.nih.gov/nia

This government agency has information for students of gerontology and family caregivers:

Administration on Aging
Washington, DC 20201
Tel: 202-619-0724
Email: aoainfo@aoa.gov
http://www.aoa.gov

Financial Planners

OVERVIEW

Financial planning is the process of establishing financial goals and creating ways to reach them. Certified *financial planners* examine the assets of their clients and suggest what steps they need to take in the future to meet their goals. They take a broad approach to financial advice, which distinguishes them from other professional advisers, such as insurance agents, stockbrokers, accountants, attorneys, and real estate agents, each of whom typically focuses on only one aspect of a person's finances.

HISTORY

Except for the depression years of the 1930s, the United States economy expanded almost without interruption after World War I. As the average American's income increased, so did lifestyle expectations. By the 21st century, vacations to Disney World, cell phones for everyone in the family, two or three cars in the garage, and thoughts of a financially worry-free retirement were not uncommon occurrences or beliefs. But how do Americans meet such high expectations? More and more have begun turning to professionals—financial planners—who recommend financial strategies. Fee-only financial planners, so called because they charge a flat fee instead of a commission or some other form of payment, represent a growing segment of the financial advising industry, but the profession as a whole is booming due to the deregulation of certain institutions dealing with money. Because of this deregulation, banks, brokerage firms, and insurance companies have been allowed to offer more financial services—

including investment advice—to customers since 1999. This has created many job openings for planners who want to work for these businesses.

Other reasons for growth in this industry include the large number of people (baby boomers, born between 1946 and 1964) who are closing in on or reaching retirement age and taking stock of their assets. As boomers consider if they have enough money to pay for the retirement they want, more and more of them are turning to financial planners for advice about such things as annuities, long-term health insurance, and individual retirement accounts. Another factor that has spurred growth is the increased awareness people have about investing and other options because of the large amount of financial information now directed at the general public. Today commercials for brokerage firms, television talk shows with weekly money advice, and financial publications and websites all offer various news and tips about what the average person should do with his or her money. All this information can be overwhelming, and people are turning to experts for help. As tax laws change, the world economy becomes more complex, and new technologies alter workforces, financial planners will continue to be in demand for their expert advice.

THE JOB

Financial planners advise their clients on many aspects of finance. Although they seem to be jacks of all trades, certified financial planners do not work alone; they meet with their clients' other advisers, such as attorneys, accountants, trust officers, and investment bankers. Financial planners fully research their clients' overall financial picture. After meeting with the clients and their other advisers, certified financial planners analyze the data they have received and generate a written report that includes their recommendations on how the clients can best achieve their goals. This report details the clients' financial objectives, current income, investments, risk tolerance, expenses, tax returns, insurance coverage, retirement programs, estate plans, and other important information.

Financial planning is an ongoing process. The plan must be monitored and reviewed periodically so that adjustments can be made, if necessary, to assure that it continues to meet individual needs.

The plan itself is a set of recommendations and strategies for clients to use or ignore, according to The Princeton Review Online, and financial planners should be ready to answer hard questions about the integrity of the plans they map out. After all, they are dealing with all of the money and investments that their clients have worked a lifetime to accrue.

People need financial planners for different things. Some might want life insurance, college savings plans, or estate planning. Sometimes these needs are triggered by changes in people's lives, such as retirement, death of a spouse, disability, marriage, birth of children, or job changes. Certified financial planners spend the majority of their time on the following topics: investment planning, retirement planning, tax planning, estate planning, and risk management. All of these areas require different types of financial knowledge, and planners are generally expected to be extremely competent in the disciplines of asset management, employee benefits, estate planning, insurance, investments, and retirement, according to the Institute of Certified Financial Planners. A financial planner must also have good interpersonal skills, since establishing solid client-planner relationships is essential to the planner's success. It also helps to have good communication skills, since even the best financial plan, if presented poorly to a client, can be rejected.

The job of financial planners is driven by clients. The advice planners provide depends on their clients' particular needs, resources, and priorities. Many people think they cannot afford or do not need a comprehensive financial plan. Certified financial planners must have a certain amount of expertise in sales to build their client base.

Certified financial planners use various ways to develop their client lists, including telephone solicitation, giving seminars on financial planning to the general public or specific organizations, and networking with social contacts. Referrals from satisfied customers also help the business grow.

Although certified financial planners are trained in comprehensive financial planning, some specialize in one area, such as asset management, investments, or retirement planning. In most small or self-owned financial planning companies, they are generalists. However, in some large companies, planners might specialize in particular areas, including insurance, real estate, mutual funds, annuities, pensions, or business valuations.

REQUIREMENTS

High School

If financial planning sounds interesting to you, take as many business classes as possible as well as mathematics. Communication courses, such as speech or drama, will help put you at ease when talking in front of a crowd, something financial planners must do occasionally. English courses will help you prepare the written reports planners present to their clients.

Postsecondary Training

Earning a bachelor's degree starts financial planners on the right track, but it will help if your degree indicates a skill with numbers, be it in science or business. A business administration degree with a specialization in financial planning or a liberal arts degree with courses in accounting, business administration, economics, finance, marketing, human behavior, counseling, and public speaking is excellent preparation for this sort of job.

Certification or Licensing

Education alone will not motivate clients to easily turn over their finances to you. Many financial professionals must be licensed on the state and federal levels in financial planning specialties, such as stocks and insurance. The Securities and Exchange Commission and most states have licensing requirements for investment advisers, a category under which most financial planners also fall. However, most of the activities of planners are not regulated by the government. Therefore, to show credibility to clients, most financial planners choose to become certified as either a certified financial planner [CFP(R)] or a chartered financial consultant (ChFC).

To receive the CFP(R) mark of certification, offered by the Certified Financial Planner Board of Standards, candidates must meet educational requirements, pass a comprehensive examination, and follow an enforceable code of ethics.

The American College in Bryn Mawr, Pa., offers the ChFC designation. To receive this designation, candidates must complete eight courses stipulated by The American College, meet experience requirements, and agree to uphold The American College's Code of Ethics and Procedures.

To maintain the CFP and the ChFC designations, professionals will need to meet continuing-education and other requirements as determined by the CFP Board and The American College.

Other Requirements

Other factors that contribute to success as a financial planner include keeping up with continuing education, referrals from clients, specialization, people and communication skills, and a strong educational background.

EXPLORING

Success as a certified financial planner comes only with training and years on the job. However, you can check out the financial planning information available on the Internet to familiarize yourself with the terms used in the industry. You should also take as many finance and business classes as possible. Talking to certified financial planners will also help you gather information on the field. Performing an internship or getting a part-time or summer job in an accounting, auditing, or financial planning firm will provide valuable experience for this career.

EMPLOYERS

According to the U.S. Department of Labor, 38 percent of financial planners and advisers are self-employed. About 31 percent are employed by securities and commodities brokers, exchanges, and investment services firms. A smaller, but growing, number of financial planners are employed by corporations, banks, credit unions, mutual fund companies, insurance companies, accounting or law firms, colleges and universities, and credit counseling organizations.

STARTING OUT

Early in their careers, financial planners work for banks, mutual fund companies, or investment firms and usually receive extensive on-the-job training. The job will deal heavily with client-based and research activities. Financial planners may start their own business as they learn personal skills and build their client base. During the first few years, certified financial planners spend many hours analyzing documents, meeting with other advisers, and networking to find new clients.

ADVANCEMENT

Those who have not changed their career track in five years can expect to have established some solid, long-term relationships with clients. Measured success at this point will be the planners' service fees, which will be marked up considerably from when they started their careers.

Those who have worked in the industry for 10 years usually have many clients, a good track record, and a six-figure income. Experienced financial planners can also move into careers in investment banking, financial consulting, and financial analysis. Because people skills are also an integral part of being a financial planner, consulting, on both personal and corporate levels, is also an option. Many planners will find themselves attending business school, either to achieve a higher income or to switch to one of the aforementioned professions.

EARNINGS

There are several methods of compensation for financial planners. Fee-only means that compensation is earned entirely from fees from consultation, plan development, or investment management. These fees may be charged on an hourly or project basis depending on clients' needs or on a percentage of assets under management. Commission-only compensation is received from the sale of financial products that clients agree to purchase to implement financial planning recommendations. There is no charge for advice or preparation of the financial plan. Fee-offset means that compensation received in the form of commission from the sale of financial products is offset against fees charged for the planning process. Combination fee/commission is a fee charged for consultation, advice, and financial plan preparation on an hourly, project, or percentage basis. Planners might also receive commissions from recommended products targeted to achieve goals and objectives. Some planners work on a salary basis for financial services institutions such as banks, credit unions, and other related organizations.

The U.S. Department of Labor reports that financial planners earned a median annual salary of $56,680 in 2002. The middle 50 percent of financial planners made between $36,180 and $100,540.

The median hourly rate for financial planners was $150 in 2003, according to the 2003 Survey of Trends in Financial Planning, conducted by the College for Financial Planning in Greenwood Village, Colorado. The same survey found that median gross earnings for planners with 21–25 years of experience were $203,000.

Firms might provide beginning financial planners with a steady income by paying a draw, which is a minimum salary based on the commission and fees the planner can be expected to earn. Some financial planners receive vacation days, sick days, and health insurance, but that depends on whether they work for financial institutions or on their own.

WORK ENVIRONMENT

Most financial planners work by themselves in offices or at home. Others work in offices with other financial planners. Established financial planners usually work the same hours as others in the business community. Beginners who are seeking customers probably work longer hours. Many planners accommodate customers by meeting with them in the evenings and on weekends. They might spend a lot of time out of the office meeting with current and prospective clients, attending civic functions, and participating in trade association meetings.

OUTLOOK

The employment of financial planners is expected to grow faster than the average through 2012. More funds should be available for investment, as the economy, personal income, and inherited wealth grow. Demographics will also play a role; as increasing numbers of baby boomers turn 50, demand will grow for retirement-related investments. Most people, in general, are likely to turn to financial planners for assistance with retirement planning. Individual saving and investing for retirement are expected to become more important, as many companies reduce pension benefits and switch from defined-benefit retirement plans to defined-contribution plans such as 401(k) accounts, which shift the investment responsibility from the company to the individual. Furthermore, a growing number of individual investors are expected to seek advice from financial planners regarding the increasing complexity and array of investment alternatives for assistance with estate planning.

Due to the highly competitive nature of financial planning, many beginners leave the field because they are not able to establish a sufficient clientele. Once established, however, planners have a strong attachment to their occupation because of high earning potential and considerable investment in training. Job opportunities should be best for mature individuals with successful work experience and professional certification.

FOR MORE INFORMATION

For more information about financial education and the ChFC designation, contact
The American College
270 South Bryn Mawr Avenue
Bryn Mawr, PA 19010
Tel: 888-263-7265
http://www.amercoll.edu

To learn more about financial planning and to obtain a copy of the Guide to CFP Certification, *contact*
Certified Financial Planner Board of Standards
1670 Broadway, Suite 600
Denver, CO 80290-4809
Tel: 888-237-6275
Email: initialcert@cfp-board.org
http://www.cfp-board.org

For information on educational opportunities and to read a glossary of financial terms, visit the following website:
College for Financial Planning
6161 South Syracuse Way
Greenwood Village, CO 80111-4707
Tel: 800-237-9990
Email: enroll@fp.edu
http://www.fp.edu

For more information on fee-only financial advisors, contact
National Association of Personal Financial Advisors
3250 North Arlington Heights Road, Suite 109
Arlington Heights, IL 60004
Tel: 888-366-2732
Email: info@napfa.org
http://www.napfa.org

Geriatric Care Managers

OVERVIEW

Geriatric care managers are professionals who specialize in assisting older people and their families in meeting short-term and long-term care needs. Care managers may coordinate a senior's schedule by making and taking the senior to their doctor's appointments; they may help seniors and their families find an appropriate place for the older person to live; and they may help the older person keep track of finances or recommend someone who is qualified to do this. In general, care managers provide older people with a vital link to the outside world. At the same time, they serve as a link from younger family members who may live in a different city to the senior family member. Geriatric care managers typically have training in gerontology, social work, nursing, or counseling.

HISTORY

The elderly must deal with changes that may include diminished hearing or sight, an inability to remember certain events, loss of the ability to concentrate for extended periods of time, and reduced physical strength. Historically, a long life was only possible for those who had the means and support systems to provide for their own care late in life. Disease and natural threats severely limited the life spans of middle- and lower-class people; only the wealthy were shielded from the more acute threats to their lives.

Over the centuries, advances in medicine, technologies, education, and other fields have combined to dramatically improve the conditions of the average person's life, and, as a result, life spans have greatly increased. In the United States today, there are more senior citizens than at any other time in our history, and that number continues to increase. The U.S. Census Bureau predicts that the population age 65 and over will more than double by 2050 (increasing from approximately 35 million in 2000 to 82 million in 2050). In addition, the number of people age 85 or older may more than quadruple by 2050 (increasing from approximately 4 million in 2000 to 19 million in 2050). A study by the National Alliance for Caregiving projects that approximately 10 percent of all employed people will be working as paid caregivers by the end of the first decade of the 21st century.

Traditionally, several generations of one family (grandparents, parents, children) lived in the same area. One benefit of this arrangement was that it made it possible for family members to easily care for each other. By the last decades of the 20th century, however, generations of one family were quite frequently living apart. It had become common for elderly parents to be living in one city while their adult children lived several hundred, if not several thousand, miles away in another location. This situation, obviously, made it difficult to care for elderly parents. In other cases in which the elderly parent and adult child still lived in the same area, the adult child often had difficulty managing his or her personal and professional life as well as trying to cope with an elderly parent's needs. The adult child may not have even known about resources in the area that were available to senior citizens. Geriatric care management is a profession that developed when a handful of caring and entrepreneurial individuals began to recognize this niche needed to be filled. The profession of geriatric care manager was all but unknown until the 1980s. The National Association of Professional Geriatric Care Managers (commonly known as GCM) reports that between 1984 and 1998, the number of geriatric care managers grew from just 30 to over 1,300. In the 21st century, the need for geriatric care managers should increase steadily as the number of senior citizens grows and as families struggle to juggle the demands of children, careers, and elderly parents.

THE JOB

Geriatric care managers coordinate the many aspects of caring for the elderly. They must be able to assess the changing needs of their clients and find the best solutions to the daily problems with which they are

Words to Know

adult day care center: center featuring structured programs, usually during weekdays, that may include activities, meals, and health and rehabilitative services for the elderly in a supervised setting; transportation is sometimes included in the fee

assisted living: facility that provides individual living units, which may or may not have a kitchenette; the facility offers 24-hour, on-site response staff; additional nursing or home care services can be provided at an additional fee

companion: provides assistance with shopping, meal preparation, escort, companionship, and home upkeep; no personal care or nursing care is provided

conservator: person appointed by the court in a legal proceeding to act as the legal representative of a person who is mentally or physically incapable of managing his or her own affairs

emergency response systems: allows for 24-hour monitoring and response to medical or other emergencies

guardianship: similar to a conservatorship yet severely restricts the legal rights of an elder based on a court's finding of legal incompetence

home health care agency: agency providing medical care in the home; services can include nursing; occupational, speech, or physical therapy; social work; or a home health aide; medicare usually only covers this care during an acute period of illness

long-term care insurance: privately paid policy that provides money for pre-determined health care costs after policyholder meets certain medical requirements

Medicaid/medical assistance: federal and state government program in which the states provide health care for low-income people

Medicare: federal program providing health care coverage/insurance for people over 65 and some people with disabilities; Part A covers inpatient care, skilled nursing facility, hospice, and short-term health care; Part B covers doctors' services, outpatient hospital care, and durable medical equipment; does not provide for long-term care of the elderly except under limited conditions

power of attorney: legal document allowing one person to act in a legal matter on another's behalf

respite: time off designed to relieve the caregiver from caregiving duties either in the home, community setting, or care facility presented. This career was born in response to our large and growing elderly population, the needs of families who are caring for elderly members, and the numerous and complex health care plans available today.

Geriatric care managers perform tasks that are similar to some done by social workers, counselors, advocates, and family members. Their duties, depending on the individual, can include providing full-scale assessments of a client's needs, seeing to it that their clients take their medications and make it to scheduled doctors' appointments, taking clients grocery shopping, and providing other family members with written reports detailing how the client is doing. Mainly, though, their role is that of a coordinator. Care managers understand the health care system as well as know about services, such as Meals on Wheels or dog walking, social activities for seniors, and other such resources in their area. It is their job to put clients in touch with the services that they need.

A geriatric care manager's day might include time spent on the phone arranging services for a client; touching base with a client's family members; assisting a client with making a move from a current home to one that provides a higher level of care; conducting an assessment of a new client to determine his or her needs; talking with a bank trust officer about a client's increased care needs; accompanying a client on a trip to the emergency room; or monitoring plans and services. One of a care manager's most important tasks is to help simplify and explain options to clients and assist them and their families in making informed decisions about their health management.

Many geriatric care managers are called upon by family members who live at too great a distance to continue to assist and care for their parents. Known as the "sandwich generation," these adults are struggling to both raise their children and take care of their aging parents. These are often two-career couples and neither the wife nor the husband can leave their work on a regular basis or for long periods to take care of an elderly parent's needs, such as going to the dentist one day and an optometrist's appointment the next. In these circumstances, a trusted, reliable professional who assists in taking care of the elderly person's needs can make a big difference in quality of life, for both the elderly person and the other family members.

One of geriatric care managers' most valuable attributes is that they are educated, experienced, informed resources who understand the range of services available and have the knowledge and savvy to navigate any red tape involved. They are able to assess a client's medical needs, mental health, financial situation, legal needs, medications, physical limitations, and family and community support. They are experts in the wide range of services available to the elderly, and they recommend services based upon each client's means and needs. They find assistance that meets the client's needs but does not exceed their resources, financially, emotionally, or physically. In so doing, geriatric care managers not only help contain expenses for their clients but also help ensure the elderly person remains as independent as possible.

Usually, care managers get new clients when a family is faced with a crisis involving an elderly member and seeks out help. While it's not preferable to make decisions in emotionally charged situations, a crisis is often the impetus that spurs a family into action. Often this situation is complicated because the family feels that some kind of intervention is needed, but the elderly person might feel everything is fine and not want help.

Many times families on tight budgets have simple needs in mind when they contact a care manager. For example, they might call on a geriatric care manager to help an elderly member take care of tasks such as getting the house painted or taking a pet to the veterinarian. Such help allows the older person to remain at home for as long as possible, which is a financial advantage as well as a lifestyle preference. Such an arrangement also provides peace of mind to other family members.

Geriatric care managers must also do a lot of paperwork, keeping up-to-date files on their clients, scheduling meetings, and writing reports to families. And since many care managers are in business for themselves, they must also do a number of administrative tasks. These tasks include recordkeeping for the business, billing clients, managing the business's finances, and doing advertising or marketing work to attract new clients. Clearly, the geriatric care manager must be comfortable taking on many responsibilities.

The significance of this job should not be underestimated. Geriatric care managers hold positions of great importance, and their work benefits society, the elderly, and the families involved. It should be noted that this work can take an emotional toll, as care managers must deal with their feelings about the inevitable decline and death of their clients. Nevertheless, many find this a rewarding career, knowing that they are working to improve the lives of the elderly.

REQUIREMENTS
High School
You should take a college preparatory curriculum, and, because many skills are necessary to be an effective geriatric care manager, there are plenty of classes you can take to help prepare you for this work.

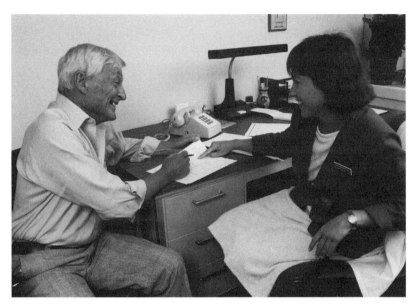

Geriatric care managers must form good relationships with their clients so they can assess their changing needs. *(Getty Images)*

Classes in health are an obvious choice; geriatric care managers need to have an understanding of the human body and how its functions are affected by the aging process. Psychology courses are helpful, since you will need to understand and deal with a variety of people in a myriad of circumstances. Courses in sociology can introduce you to yet another aspect of the geriatric and health care realm. Sciences, such as biology and chemistry, are also useful. Don't neglect your math studies, since you may need to deal with clients' financial questions as well as keep your own records regarding billing and expenses. You will also benefit from English or communication courses, as it will be imperative that you can convey information effectively to your clients and their families.

Postsecondary Training
There are a number of career paths you can take to enter this field. Geriatric care managers usually have a minimum of a bachelor's degree in a field such as nursing, psychology, gerontology, or social work, and many also have master's degrees. While you are in college, therefore, you should consider majoring in one of these subjects, and the courses you take will fulfill the requirements for that major. Those interested in nursing may have classes such as human growth and development, pathophysiology, and pharmacotherapeutics, for exam-

ple, while those pursuing a bachelor's degree in social work may take classes in social welfare policies, human behavior and social environments, and a field practicum. In addition, take any courses that focus on the elderly in order to get an understanding of their needs and situations. Some people begin working after college with the goal of becoming involved with elderly clients to gain experience before setting up their own care management business. In some cases, local geriatric care management services may offer internships, and this may be another way to gain experience.

Those who go on to get master's degrees will take advanced courses in their field of interest. For example, nurses in master's programs focusing on gerontology may take classes such as older adults in primary care, advanced health assessment, and medical legal issues; those in master's programs in social work may take courses such as sociobehavioral theory and social work methods; and so forth. Like people with bachelor's degrees, those with master's degrees may begin working at a job in their general field (nursing, psychology, social work, etc.) while trying to get as much exposure to geriatric clientele as they can. This allows them to gain experience and make contacts before they begin their independent careers as geriatric care managers.

Certification or Licensing

The National Academy of Certified Care Managers has been administering a certification program since 1997. Those who meet requirements and pass a written test receive the designation care manager, certified (CMC). Although having the CMC is not yet commonplace, it may become more popular as this field grows.

Currently, no licensing exists for geriatric care managers as such. Those who have a background in a field requiring licensing, such as nursing, social work, or psychology, are licensed in that field.

Other Requirements

Geriatric care management is a field that requires a lot of the so-called "soft skills;" compassion, responsibility, patience, and ethics are some of the more obvious characteristics. Assertiveness is also important, as you will be acting as an advocate for your clients, going to whatever lengths necessary to get your client what he or she needs and deserves. A professional demeanor is important, as you will be dealing with attorneys, trust officers, care providers, and other professionals, as well as the client's concerned family members or friends. Good judgment and assessment skills are a necessity. You should also have extensive knowledge of health care issues and the resources that are available to your clients. You will need to maintain a calm disposition in a crisis. You might find yourself accompanying a client to the emergency room, comforting family members during bad times, or visiting clients in what can be disturbing environments. You should be a people person, able to form long-term relationships with clients and their families, because your role will be one of great importance to them.

EXPLORING

You might find it informative to talk to your parents about the current and future needs of older relatives. These matters are best approached with some sensitivity, as you may encounter reluctance to discuss the topic. Being able to extend empathy and compassion is another key characteristic of a successful geriatric care manager, so this is an important area to explore.

It is always valuable to talk to an experienced professional in the field you are considering. Your high school guidance counselor, a local business directory, or the National Association of Professional Geriatric Care Managers may be able to provide you with leads in locating a geriatric care manager who would be willing to talk with you about the job. (See the end of this article for contact information.)

You may also find value in speaking to professionals in related fields, such as lawyers in elder law, nurses and doctors in geriatric medicine, managers of nursing homes, physical therapists, and so forth.

An excellent way to explore this field is to volunteer at a geriatric program or facility. Working with the elderly can be very rewarding, and you will have the opportunity to talk directly with many older people. Being able to relate to those of a different generation is a key skill of this job.

You can also volunteer at a nursing home or extended care facility. This work can be more challenging, but it will afford you the opportunity to discover your ability to work with those with failing mental and physical capacities in the context of their living environment.

EMPLOYERS

The majority of geriatric care managers are employed in private practice. Others are employed by elder care service organizations, adult day care centers, elder abuse programs, banks, and other institutions or businesses that have dealings with older people. Some faith-based agencies, such as the Council for Jewish Elderly, also offer geriatric care management. Any of these might be potential employers; even individual practitioners may be likely to hire assistants and caregiving aides.

Health maintenance organizations do not currently pay for geriatric care management services. As the population ages and the collective voice of senior citizens grows louder, we may see more subsidized care management for the elderly. Managed-care organizations are beginning to recognize that geriatric care managers play a key role in cost control. Geriatric care managers' services in promoting their clients' health, safety, and overall well-being save managed-care organizations money by lowering the occurrence of such things as small illnesses, which, left untreated, become major illnesses requiring hospitalizations.

Geriatric care managers can work in numerous places across the country. Many jobs will be clustered around major metropolitan areas, but opportunities will exist virtually anywhere.

STARTING OUT

One method of becoming a geriatric care manager is to work in a related field, such as social work, nursing, or nursing home management, before moving on to a care manager career. Jobs in these areas will give you experience and allow you to interact with those who are already geriatric care managers. In this way you can build up your resume, make connections at various agencies, learn about local resources, and perhaps even begin establishing a clientele for your own business as a geriatric care manager.

Another possibility is to start out working for another care manager who is already established in the field. This will allow you to learn the job at your own pace and gradually step up to the full duties of the job. You will have the opportunity to provide services to existing clients within the limits of your abilities. As you learn and grow, the geriatric care manager may allow you to take on more and more of the duties of your intended career. In this way you will also gain experience and make contacts that will ultimately help you develop your own clientele.

A third option is to work with your school's career placement center, which may have job listings or receive notices from agencies about openings. In addition, consider joining a professional organization, such as the National Association of Professional Geriatric Care Managers. This will help you keep up to date on topics important to those working with the elderly and give you an excellent opportunity to network with professionals.

ADVANCEMENT

Advancement options depend to a large extent on each geriatric care manager's goals. For example, those who work as assistants to other care managers or those who are part of a business with several care managers may want to advance by starting their own management service. Those with their own care management services may advance by establishing an excellent reputation and increasing their clientele. A sizeable client base, in turn, will boost the business's earnings; additionally, the care managers may then raise their fees for their in-demand services. On the other hand, some geriatric care managers who have their own businesses may consider it an advancement to form a partnership with other care managers. One benefit of this would be that each manager could concentrate on the areas of care management he or she enjoys the most. Another possibility is for a geriatric care manager in solo private practice to move to a different work setting; for example, a manager may leave solo practice to work for an organization, such as a faith-based group, that provides geriatric care management. And, naturally, this situation could be reversed: a manager could move from a job with an organization to a job in private practice.

No matter what route to advancement geriatric care managers choose, the key factors to their success will be having a reputation for doing excellent work, keeping their knowledge about laws, finances, medications, and services up to date, and enjoying working with and for the elderly.

EARNINGS

Earnings in this field vary widely with experience and geographical location. Those who are in private practice tend to charge an hourly rate. This rate can vary depending, again, on the manager's location (small town, big city, East Coast, Midwest, etc.), the manager's experience and education (those with master's degrees and several years of experience are typically able to charge higher rates), and the service the manager is providing. According to an article in the *Chicago Tribune* in 2000, geriatric care managers had a salary range of $25,000 to $100,000.

In the Washington, D.C., area, general hourly rates in 2000 ranged from $50 to $150 per hour, reports *The Washington Post*. Someone just starting out in private practice may have a small number of clients and only manage to bill for 15 or 20 hours a week. Naturally, a manager's workload will directly affect earnings; the more hours a manager can bill for, the higher the annual earnings.

The *Occupational Outlook Handbook* reports median annual salaries of $56,320 for health services managers who work in the field of home health care (a related occupation).

A typical client will require an initial period of more intense activity on the manager's part to assess his or her needs and set up services. This will often be a crisis-driven event, possibly requiring last-minute travel and other arrangements. Following this, the client will typically require less of a care manager's time each month to maintain services and periodically reassess needs.

A majority of geriatric care managers must provide for their own benefits, as so many are self-employed. Those who work for larger organizations might earn lower wages than independent consultants, but they will likely have a range of benefits such as health insurance, vacation and sick days, and retirement plans.

WORK ENVIRONMENT

Geriatric care managers spend a significant amount of time with their clients, both in their homes and in nursing facilities. The quality of these environments can range from pleasant to disturbing, depending on the condition of the client. Typically, however, managers work in quiet, indoor environments. Managers frequently need to communicate with other professionals while coordinating a client's medical, legal, and everyday needs, so much telephone work is involved. Depending on the size or the business or organization, managers may supervise and help out with the work of others. Schedules may be quite busy one day with unexpected emergencies, such as a client falling and going to the hospital, and quiet the next day with recordkeeping, phone calls, and paperwork. Many geriatric care managers are on call, available to their clients at all times for sudden needs.

This line of work can be emotionally challenging. A successful geriatric care manager will need to be able to handle anger, grief, frustration, and confusion. Conflict and stress can also occur, as care managers have to defend the rights of their clients, sometimes against the wishes of the clients' families and friends.

OUTLOOK

Geriatric care management is a fairly new profession, and, as such, the U.S. Department of Labor does not have specific employment outlook information for geriatric care managers. However, the more general category of human service worker is expected to grow much faster than the average for all occupations through 2012. Job opportunities in the field of geriatric care management are excellent, especially for those with advanced education.

In many aspects, this job represents the replacement of a traditional family function, that of caring for the elderly. As people live longer, as families typically become geographically separated, and as health insurance becomes more complicated, the need for geriatric care managers has grown dramatically. Experts predict this need only to grow in the 21st century.

FOR MORE INFORMATION

This government agency has press releases, resources for students of gerontology, and news for family caregivers. For information, contact
Administration on Aging
Washington, DC 20201
Tel: 202-619-0724
Email: aoainfo@aoa.gov
http://www.aoa.gov

For information on continuing education programs, job listings, and student resources, check out the following website:
American Society on Aging
833 Market Street, Suite 511
San Francisco, CA 94103-1824
Tel: 800-537-9728
Email: info@asaging.org
http://www.asaging.org

For information on certification, contact
National Academy of Certified Care Managers
PO Box 669
244 Upton Road
Colchester, CT 06415-0669
Tel: 800-962-2260
Email: naccm@snet.net
http://www.naccm.net

For information for both family and professional caregivers, contact
National Alliance for Caregiving
4720 Montgomery Lane, 5th Floor
Bethesda, MD 20814
Email: info@caregiving.org
http://www.caregiving.org

For information on the career, membership, how to find a care manager, and other related topics, contact
National Association of Professional Geriatric Care Managers
1604 North Country Club Road
Tucson, AZ 85716-3102
Tel: 520-881-8008
http://www.caremanager.org

For a wealth of information on topics relevant to seniors, contact
National Council on the Aging
300 D Street, SW, Suite 801
Washington, DC 20024
Tel: 202-479-1200
Email: info@ncoa.org
http://www.ncoa.org

For news releases and information on resources such as The Resource Directory for Older People, *check out the following website:*
National Institute on Aging
Building 31, Room 5C27
31 Center Drive, MSC 2292
Bethesda, MD 20892
Tel: 301-496-1752
http://www.nih.gov/nia

For information on schools and social work that focuses on work with the elderly, contact
Strengthening Aging and Gerontology Education for Social Work
Council on Social Work Education
1725 Duke Street, Suite 500
Alexandria, VA 22314
Tel: 703-683-8080
Email: aging@cswe.org
http://www.cswe.org/sage-sw

Geriatricians

QUICK FACTS

School Subjects
Biology
Chemistry

Personal Skills
Helping/teaching
Technical/scientific

Work Environment
Primarily indoors
Primarily multiple locations

Minimum Education Level
Medical degree

Salary Range
$95,000 to $155,530 to
$255,438+

Certification or Licensing
Required by all states

Outlook
Faster than the average

DOT
070

GOE
02.03.01

NOC
3111

O*NET-SOC
29-1069.99

OVERVIEW

A *geriatrician* is a physician with specialized knowledge in the prevention, diagnosis, treatment, and rehabilitation of disorders common to old age. The term "geriatrics" refers to the clinical aspects of aging and the comprehensive health care of older people. It is an area of medicine that focuses on health and disease in old age and is a growing medical specialty.

HISTORY

Since the time of Ancient Greece, there have been many advances in the medical field: the development of organized clinical instruction, vaccinations, sterilization procedures, and instruments such as the stethoscope, to name a few. In addition to these advances, the medical profession also saw the development of specialists, doctors who concentrate their work in specific areas such as surgery, psychiatry, or internal medicine. Geriatricians specialize in working with the elderly. The term geriatrics comes from the Greek terms *geras*, meaning old age, and *iatrikos*, meaning physician.

Geriatrics has only fairly recently become a popular, needed, and recognized specialty. Formal training in the field is relatively new. One reason for the development of this occupation is that people are now living longer. According to the U.S. Census Bureau, there were 3 million Americans age 65 or over living in 1900, but by 2000 this segment of the population had grown to about 35 million, an increase of more than 10 times. This large (and growing) number of older people has created a demand for specialized services. Geriatricians are doctors who fulfill this demand. As our elderly

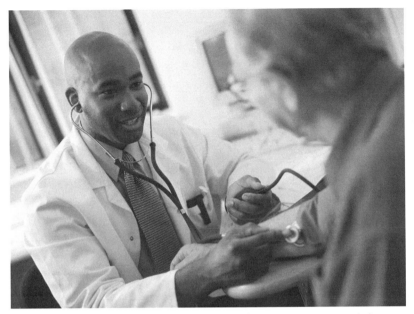

Geriatricians must have a keen interest in the aging process and the unique concerns of the elderly. *(Corbis)*

population continues to grow, geriatricians are faced with unique medical and ethical challenges in the treatment of their patients.

THE JOB

Geriatricians spend most of their time with patients, taking patient histories, listening to their comments or symptoms, and running any of a number of diagnostic tests and evaluations, including physical examinations. Geriatricians generally see patients in a clinic, a long-term care facility, or a hospital. Each patient setting requires a unique type of patient care. Geriatricians often work with other physicians to diagnose and treat multiple problems and to provide the best possible care for each patient.

For example, an elderly man's complaint of fatigue could signal one or more of a large number of disorders. Diagnosis may be complicated by the coexistence of physical and mental problems, such as heart disease and dementia (mental confusion). This may mean consulting with a psychiatrist to treat the dementia and a cardiologist for the heart problems. Not only do geriatricians work with other medical personnel, they also work with family members and community services. Very often geriatricians work with the patient's family in order to get an accurate diagnosis, proper care, and follow-up treatment. If the patient is living alone, the geriatrician might also need the support of a social worker, neighbor, or relative to make certain that proper medication is administered and that the patient is monitored. If there is no cure for the patient's condition, the geriatrician must devise some way of helping the patient cope with the condition.

The job can be emotionally demanding and frustrating, as well as rewarding. Paperwork is also a large part of geriatricians' jobs as they must complete forms, sign releases, write prescriptions, and meet the requirements of Medicare and private insurance companies.

REQUIREMENTS

High School

To become a doctor, you will need to devote many years to schooling before you are admitted to practice. Your first step, therefore, should be to take a college preparatory curriculum while in high school. Take four years of math, English, and science classes. Biology, chemistry, and physics are particularly important to take. Study a foreign language and, if your high school offers it, take Latin. Many medical terms you will encounter later on have roots in the Latin language. In addition, round out your education with history courses and courses such as psychology and sociology, which may give you a greater understanding of people, an asset in this people-oriented career.

Postsecondary Training

To become a geriatrician, you will need to earn a college degree and a medical degree, complete specialized training, and become licensed. You will need to get your bachelor's degree from an accredited college or university. Most students considering medical school get their degree in a science field. Some schools offer a premed program, which you can also take. In either case, typical studies include biology, organic and inorganic chemistry, physics, and mathematics. Competition for admission to medical school is strong. You will need to take the Medical College Admission Test as part of the admission requirements. Medical school lasts four years and students complete classroom and laboratory work as well as work with patients under the supervision of doctors and residents. After students have completed this phase of their education, they get more training through a residency, with study in a specialty area. Geriatric care is generally considered a subspecialty. So students complete their residency in one specialty area, such as internal medicine, and then go on to complete a fellowship in geriatric care. The length of these programs varies, and they can take anywhere from one to four years to complete. The Association for Gerontology in Higher Education publishes the *Directory of Educational Programs in Gerontology and Geriatrics*, which has information on more than 750 educational programs available at various levels, including fellowship programs.

Certification or Licensing

A certificate of added qualifications (CAQ) in geriatric medicine or geriatric psychiatry is offered through the certifying boards in family practice, internal medicine, osteopathic medicine, and psychiatry for physicians who have completed a fellowship program in geriatrics.

In addition, all physicians must be licensed to practice. After receiving the M.D. degree, new physicians are required to take a licensing examination conducted through the board of medical examiners in each state. Some states have reciprocity agreements with other states so that a physician licensed in one state may be automatically licensed in another without being required to pass another examination. Because this is not true throughout the United States, however, the wise physician will find out about licensing procedures before planning to move.

Other Requirements

The career of a geriatrician is both intellectually and emotionally demanding. A good geriatrician needs to be able to effectively manage all aspects of a patient's problems, including social and emotional issues. Creative problem-solving skills are an asset. Geriatricians must have a general interest in aging and the problems related to growing older. They should be effective communicators and listeners and be able to work well as members of a team. And, like any doctor, geriatricians must be committed to lifelong learning, because new advances in medicine occur continuously.

EXPLORING

You can start exploring this field by reading as much as you can about the profession. Remember to visit websites of professional organizations for more career-related information. Ask your high school guidance counselor or a science teacher to arrange for a career day in which a doctor from the local community can come in and speak to your class about the work. You can also talk with your family physician to find out what medical school and the work in general is like.

One of the best introductions to a career in health care is to volunteer at a local hospital, clinic, or nursing home. In this way, it is possible to get a feel for what it's like to work around other health care professionals and patients. In some settings, such as nursing homes, you will also find out how well you like working with older people. Other volunteer opportunities exist to work with older people as well. Check with local agencies for seniors to see if there are any outreach programs you can join. In this way you'll have direct contact with the elderly. For example, you may be asked to become a "buddy" and visit with a senior on a regular basis. Again, this will help you determine how much you enjoy being around older people as well as give you the chance to discover what they have to offer.

EMPLOYERS

Geriatricians can find employment in a wide variety of settings, including hospitals, nursing homes, long-term care facilities, and managed-care offices. Some are self-employed in their own or group practices.

Geriatricians interested in teaching work at medical schools or university hospitals. There are also positions available in government agencies such as the National Institutes of Health and the Department of Veterans Affairs. Pharmaceutical companies and chemical companies are also potential employers. They may hire geriatricians to help research and develop new drugs, instruments, and procedures.

STARTING OUT

There are no shortcuts to entering the medical profession. You will need to complete all the required schooling and training and become licensed before you are ready to enter practice. When starting out, some doctors choose to open a private practice or join an established practice. Others take jobs with hospitals and managed-care facilities. Positions are also available with government agencies, such as the National Institute on Aging. Because the education period for physicians is so long, they have the time and opportunities to make many contacts in the field. These contacts are often useful when a doctor looks for employment. Doctors may also use the services of specialized job placement agencies that work only with physicians or that work only with health care professionals of all types.

ADVANCEMENT

Advancement will depend to a large extent on a geriatrician's personal interests and goals. Some with experience may become medical directors of long-term care facilities or the heads of geriatrics divisions of HMOs. Those who are interested in teaching can advance through the ranks to hold full professorships. Geriatricians in private practice can advance with time and experience by building up their client base and creating a large practice. Other possibilities include moving into administration to direct nursing homes, home care programs, or chronic care facilities.

EARNINGS

Physicians have some of the highest earnings among all occupations. According to a 2002 survey conducted by the Medical Group Management Association, physicians specializing in internal medicine had average salaries of $155,530, with those in the lowest 25 percent earning $95,000 a year or less. Surgeons made an average salary of $255,438, and physicians with family practices earned $150,267. Although these are not figures specifically for geriatricians, they are comparable to what these specialists earn. Earnings are also affected by what area of the country a physician works in, type of employer, size of the practice, and even his or her reputation. A doctor who is known for being rude to patients and their families, for example, will probably not have as much business as a doctor known for being kind.

Benefits depend on the employer, but usually include standard ones such as vacation time and insurance.

WORK ENVIRONMENT

Work environments are influenced by the setting in which geriatricians work, that is, hospitals, private offices, nursing homes, or schools, for example. Any geriatrician who works with patients, however, will practice in offices and examining rooms that are well equipped, clean, attractive, well lighted, and well ventilated. Geriatricians in private practice usually see patients by appointments that are scheduled according to individual requirements. In private offices there is usually at least one nurse-receptionist, and there may be several nurses, a laboratory technician, one or more secretaries, and a bookkeeper.

Because treating an older patient can be very complicated, geriatricians usually find that they have a lot of interaction with other doctors and health care professionals as they work out treatment plans.

Geriatricians working at medical schools or doing research will also find themselves in clean, well-equipped environments. Paperwork will be part of any geriatrician's job. It may range from documenting research to completing insurance forms to filling out grade reports. The environment in any of these settings will be professional.

OUTLOOK

The U.S. Department of Labor predicts job growth for all physicians to be about as fast as the average through 2012. The outlook should be even better for those working in geriatric medicine. Today, approximately 35 million Americans are age 65 or older. This number is expected to increase to 70 million by 2030 and more than 80 million by 2050. As the large generation of baby boomers ages, more physicians will be needed to treat their specific needs. According to a July 2000 article in the *Chicago Tribune,* only 100–150 physicians each year decide to work in geriatrics. This small number of incoming specialists means the field will continue to offer numerous employment opportunities. The outlook for geriatricians should remain faster than the average for some time to come.

FOR MORE INFORMATION

The following organizations provide information on geriatrician careers:
Alzheimer's Association
225 North Michigan Avenue, Floor 17
Chicago, IL 60611-1676
Tel: 800-272-3900
Email: info@alz.org
http://www.alz.org

American Association for Geriatric Psychiatry
7910 Woodmont Avenue, Suite 1050
Bethesda, MD 20814-3004
Tel: 301-654-7850
Email: main@aagponline.org
http://www.aagpgpa.org

American Federation for Aging Research
70 West 40th Street, 11th Floor
New York, NY 10018
Tel: 212-703-9977
Email: info@afar.org
http://www.afar.org

American Geriatrics Society
350 Fifth Avenue, Suite 801
New York, NY 10118
Tel: 212-308-1414
Email: info@americangeriatrics.org
http://www.americangeriatrics.org

Association for Gerontology in
  Higher Education
1030 15th Street, NW, Suite 240
Washington, DC 20005-1503
Tel: 202-289-9806
Email: aghetemp@aghe.org
http://www.aghe.org

═══ INTERVIEW ═══

Joseph Kandel has been a licensed medical doctor since 1985. Since 1989 he has held a private practice in southwest Florida. He is predominantly a clinical neurologist and specializes in geriatric medicine. He has written a number of books, made three videos, and has lectured extensively. He is also an associate professor at Wright State University School of Medicine and has performed a number of clinical trials. Dr. Kandel spoke with the editors of Careers in Focus: Geriatric Care *about his career.*

Q. What made you decide to become a physician?

A. I have always wanted to be a doctor. Ever since the age of five I knew this is what I would do. I like the idea of helping people, and now that I have been in practice for a while, I like it even more. My field provides lots of cognitive challenges, is very rewarding, and I am paid very well. Of course, I have been labeled a work-a-holic. I usually put in 15–16 hour days Monday through Friday, I work from 7:00 A.M. to noon on Saturday, and am usually in the office doing dictation from 7:00 A.M. to noon on Sunday; that doesn't count the time I spend "on call."

Q. What attracted you to the field of geriatrics?

A. The challenge. Patients have so many interesting and complicated stories. It is rare that I see a senior adult with a "simple problem." I know that many physicians find this overwhelming. I find it exciting. When you help an 80 year old with back pain walk and live pain free; when you help a patient who has suffered a stroke recover and golf or dance again; when you slow down Parkinson's disease or Alzheimer's in a patient and add years of quality to their life, that is rewarding and exciting and fun.

Q. **Did you undertake any special courses of study to specialize in geriatric medicine?**

A. My whole residency training is geared to geriatric medicine. Certainly, continuing medical education is mandatory.

Q. **What would you say are the pros and cons of your career?**

A. I live in a relatively small town—Naples, Florida. I have practiced here for 15 years. I do love it when I or my wife go somewhere and people come over to thank me for the care I've given them or their family and loved ones. I love hearing thank you. No one likes insurance or legal battles—they are both ruining health care in this country—but helping patients through the quagmire that is our health care system is very rewarding.

Q. **What would you say are the most important skills and personal qualities for someone in your field?**

(1) Be bright. Have a good database of information at your disposal.

(2) Be interested. If you are interested, you pay attention to the details.

(3) Communicate. Make the patients *better patients*. That makes you a better doctor.

(4) Involve others. Get other doctors involved to make the diagnosis and treat the patient. Get therapists and home health professionals involved. With the permission of the patient, get family members involved.

Q. **Are there any challenges that are unique to your area of medicine?**

A. Expensive tests and medicines, but that goes with any field. Most of my patients are on multiple medicines for multiple problems. Transportation to doctor appointments, therapies, etc. can be an issue for patients.

Q. What advice would you give to someone who is interested in pursuing this type of career?

A. Volunteer. Get to know what medicine and health care are really all about. Study hard. Learn. Read. Broaden your horizons. Every life activity brings some sort of wisdom and growth.

Also, be positive. Too many people are negative about health care in this country, but it is still far and away the best in the world!

Geriatric Nurses

QUICK FACTS

School Subjects
Biology
Chemistry

Personal Skills
Helping/teaching
Technical/scientific

Work Environment
Primarily indoors
Primarily one location

Minimum Education Level
Some postsecondary training

Salary Range
$33,970 to $48,090 to
$69,670+

Certification or Licensing
Required by all states

Outlook
Much faster than the average

DOT
075

GOE
10.02.01

NOC
3152

O*NET-SOC
29-1111.00

OVERVIEW

Geriatric nurses provide direct patient care to elderly people in their homes, or in hospitals, nursing homes, and clinics. The term *geriatrics* refers to the clinical aspects of aging and the overall health care of the aging population. Since older people tend to have different reactions to illness and disease than younger people, treating them has become a specialty.

HISTORY

The specialty of gerontology nursing started developing in the 20th century as people routinely began to live longer than in past generations. Healthier lifestyles, new medicines, and new medical procedures, among other things, contributed to this change in life span. And as more and more people lived longer, a growing number needed and wanted the expertise of health care professionals who are well versed in the needs and concerns of older people. Geriatric nurses are able to address the special health problems older people may face, such as serious chronic problems (heart disease or blood pressure illness), decreases in senses and physical agility (sight, hearing, balance) that lead to injuries from accidents, and the problems that may result from accidents (learning to walk again after a broken hip).

The U.S. Census Bureau reported that in 2000, the senior population (those 65 and over) was approximately 35 million. The bureau also predicted that figure will rise steadily and projected the number of seniors living in 2050 to be approximately 82 million. Thus, health care services for seniors will continue to be a growing field.

THE JOB

According to registered nurse Jean Abdollahian, a retired geriatric nurse and nursing home administrator, "Geriatric nursing is a different kind of nursing. These patients need a special kind of nursing and they almost always need more attention."

She continues, "In many aspects, geriatric nursing parallels pediatric nursing. Some elderly patients may have illnesses of childlike qualities that demand attention, love, and special medical care." Abdollahian adds, "The caregiver must have patience and a good sense of humor to deal with many trying situations."

Geriatric nurses focus primarily on caring for elderly patients. This care may be provided in an institution, in the home as a visiting nurse or hospice nurse, in a retirement community, in a doctor's office, in the hospital, or at wellness clinics in the community. Some geriatric nurses may also give health seminars or workshops to the elderly in the community, or they may be involved in research or pilot studies that deal with health and disease among the aging population.

Geriatric nurses can expect to perform many of the skills required of any nursing professional. Many nurses who specialize in other types of care, with the exception of pediatrics and obstetrics, almost always find themselves caring for the elderly as well.

There are many nursing specialties under the broad umbrella of geriatric nursing. Abdollahian notes from her past experience, "A geriatric nurse touches on almost all aspects of nursing: from intensive care, to emergency, to cardiac, to oncology. There are specialties within the specialty."

A common geriatrics specialty is a *medications nurse,* who has additional pharmacology training. This nurse has an extensive knowledge of drugs and their effects on the elderly, and he or she oversees the administration of medications to patients. Abdollahian notes that many state and federal laws now dictate how facilities can restrain their patients either physically or medicinally, so the medications nurse must be aware of these laws and see that the facility abides by these rules.

Another type of geriatric nurse is a *charge nurse,* who oversees a particular shift of nurses and aides who care for the elderly. Although all health providers are required to do a lot of paperwork to document the care they provide and patients' progress, the charge nurse and administrators are responsible for even more documentation required by HMOs, the federal government, and insurance providers.

Advancement into administration positions such as nursing home administrator or director of nursing is common for persons involved in a geriatric nursing career.

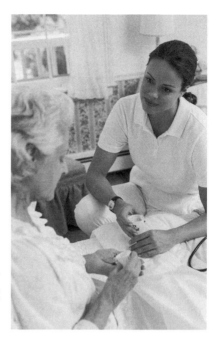

Geriatric nurses work with elderly patients in hospitals, nursing homes, and in patients' homes. *(Getty Images)*

"This is a very rewarding area of nursing," says Abdollahian. "This is a fascinating age to work with. They have gone from the horse and buggy days to seeing a man walk on the moon. They have so many stories to tell."

REQUIREMENTS

High School

If you are interested in a geriatric nursing career, be prepared to continue your education after high school. You should take a general college preparatory curriculum, which will include studies in history, social sciences, science, math, English, and computer science. Science and math classes, such as biology, chemistry, physics, algebra, and geometry, will be particularly important to take. Taking four years of English classes is also recommended because these classes will enhance your ability to research, write, and speak effectively. In addition, you should consider taking a foreign language, which will further broaden your communication skills.

Postsecondary Training

To work as a geriatric nurse, you must first become a registered nurse (RN). There are three basic kinds of training programs that you can choose from to become an RN: associate's degree programs, diploma programs, and bachelor's degree programs. The associate in arts in nursing is awarded after completion of a two-year program, which is usually offered by junior or community colleges. You receive hospital training at cooperating hospitals in the general vicinity of the community college. The diploma program, which usually lasts three years, is conducted by hospitals and independent schools.

Perhaps the best route, however, is the bachelor's degree program. One reason is that you will have more time to study a variety of topics in a four-year bachelor's program. As the need for geriatric nurses has grown, more and more bachelor's programs have begun to incorporate classes on gerontological nursing or care of older adults into their core curriculums. This degree will also provide the most career mobility, because a bachelor's degree is required for most supervisory or administrative positions, for jobs in public health agencies, and for admission to graduate nursing programs. The bachelor's of science (B.S.) in nursing is offered by colleges and universities and takes four (in some cases, five) years to complete. Besides taking courses to fulfill your college's general requirements, typical courses you may encounter in a B.S. nursing program include health assessment, pharmacology, nursing care of adults, health policy and issues, gerontological nursing, and management strategies. Once you have completed any one of these three programs, you must take and pass a licensing examination that is required in all states to become an RN.

To become a gerontological nurse, you'll need to gain experience working in gerontology, and, if you fulfill other requirements, you can become certified as a gerontological nurse by the American Nurses Credentialing Center (ANCC). If you would like to advance into a specialty position, a position with more responsibilities, or a position teaching at a college or university, you will need to pursue additional education. With a master's degree, you can work as a *gerontological nurse practitioner* or a clinical specialist in gerontological nursing. Nurses in these advanced positions are able to diagnose and treat common illnesses. In addition, they can have prescriptive authority; that is, they can write prescriptions for their patients. Nurses wanting to pursue research need to complete a doctorate degree. The National League for Nursing Accrediting Commission is responsible for accrediting all types of nursing programs offering a certificate, diploma, undergraduate, or graduate degree. The Commission on Collegiate Nursing Education, part of the American Association of Colleges of Nursing, also accredits nursing programs. Both groups provide information on these approved programs (see the end of this article for contact information).

Certification or Licensing

Certification is available from ANCC and is highly recommended. Candidates with bachelor's degrees, current RN licenses, and a certain amount of experience in the area of practice (gerontology) are eligible to take the specialty and informatics exam. Upon passing this test, they are board certified and can use the initials RN, BC after their names. Nurse practitioners and clinical specialists who fulfill certain eligibility requirements and pass an exam can become board certified as advanced practice registered nurses (APRN, BC).

All states and the District of Columbia require practicing nurses to be licensed.

Other Requirements

Geriatric nurses should enjoy working with and being around older people. They must have a general interest in aging and understand the problems related to growing older. The geriatric nurse must have the ability to get along with the patient's family members and must be able to work well with other professionals such as hospice nurses, chaplains, and social workers. Being able to work as part of a team is essential since many people may become involved in the health care and health needs of the elderly person. Communication skills are also essential. The nurse must be able to communicate with the family and the patient and explain medical terminology and procedures to them so they understand what is being done and why.

EXPLORING

You can explore your interest in nursing and in working with older people in a number of ways. Read books and visit websites that deal with the nursing profession. Ask your high school guidance counselor to help you arrange for an informational interview with a local nurse. Your school nurse is also someone to consult about the profession and the education required for it. Many hospitals have volunteer programs that provide the opportunity to work during the summer or on a part-time basis, escorting patients to tests, delivering flowers to patients' rooms, and doing other helpful tasks. Volunteering at a hospital will give you a lot of insight as to how hospitals work and how well you like this environment.

To explore how much you enjoy working with older people, volunteer at a senior center, where you may be able to sit in on a card game or teach a crafts project. Volunteer positions as well as part-time or summer jobs also may be available at a nursing home in your area. Use any opportunity you can to visit with older people in your community. You will learn a lot from being around them, and they may be just as eager to learn something from you.

EMPLOYERS

Geriatric nurses work in a variety of settings, depending on their education and personal goals. Many geriatric nurses work in nursing homes, hospitals, retirement communities, or clinics. They may also work in hospice and home care or community nursing programs; others work in private offices for gerontologists or at government agencies. Nurses who teach or do research are most often in academic settings, usually in buildings that are well-lighted, comfortable, and busy.

STARTING OUT

Once you have become a registered nurse, you can apply directly to hospitals, nursing homes, government agencies, and other organizations that hire nurses and offer opportunities to work with older patients. In addition, your school's placement office should have information on job openings. Nurses' associations and their websites, professional journals, and newspapers also frequently advertise open positions.

ADVANCEMENT

Advancement in this field often comes with further education. Those with bachelor's degrees can obtain graduate degrees and work as gerontological nurse practitioners or clinical specialists in gerontological nursing. These nurses have greater responsibilities and command higher salaries. Other specialties, such as medications nurse and charge nurse, also require advanced education. Nurses who obtain additional education in administration and management may move into administration positions at nursing departments, hospitals, or nursing homes.

EARNINGS

According to the U.S. Department of Labor's *Occupational Outlook Handbook,* registered nurses earned a median salary of $48,090 in 2002. The lowest paid 10 percent earned less than $33,970, while the middle 50 percent earned between $40,140 and $57,490. The top 10 percent made over $69,670 a year. However, geriatric specialty nurses can generally expect to earn more, especially when advancing to administrative positions.

Salary is determined by many factors, including nursing specialty, education, and place of employment, shift worked, geographical location, and work experience. Flexible schedules and part-time employment opportunities are available for most nurses. Employers usually provide health and life insurance, and some offer educational reimbursements and year-end bonuses to their full-time staff.

WORK ENVIRONMENT

Geriatric nurses can expect to work in a variety of settings depending on their nursing responsibilities. Many geriatric nurses work in nursing homes, hospitals, retirement communities, or in clinics. They may also work with hospice and community nursing programs, or as office nurses for gerontologists.

Although most health care environments will be clean and well lighted there may be some nursing situations where the surroundings may be less than desirable or where safety may be an issue.

All nursing careers have some health and disease risks; however, adherence to health and safety guidelines greatly minimizes the chance of contracting infectious diseases such as hepatitis and AIDS. Medical knowledge and good safety measures are also needed to limit the nurse's exposure to toxic chemicals, radiation, and other hazards.

OUTLOOK

Nursing specialties will be in great demand in the future. The U.S. Bureau of Labor Statistics predicts that there will be more new jobs for registered nurses than for any other career through 2012. Most of these jobs will result from current nurses reaching retirement age, in addition to the many technological advances in medicine that will create a need for more people to administer patient care.

Job opportunities for individuals who enter geriatric nursing is predicted to grow at a rate much faster than the average. The U.S. Bureau of the Census estimates that the number of individuals aged 65 or older will double by 2050. As the older population increases, their need for medical care will also increase. In addition, a 2001 report by the Nursing Institute at the University of Illinois predicts that the ratio of caregivers to the elderly population will decrease by 40 percent between 2010 and 2030. As a result, employment prospects for qualified geriatric nurses are nearly limitless.

FOR MORE INFORMATION

For more information on geriatric nursing and nursing careers in general, contact the following organizations:

American Association of Colleges of Nursing
One Dupont Circle, NW, Suite 530
Washington, DC 20036
Tel: 202-463-6930
http://www.aacn.nche.edu

American Association of Critical Care Nurses
101 Columbia
Aliso Viejo, CA 92656-4109
Tel: 800-899-2226
Email: info@aacn.org
http://www.aacn.org

American Geriatrics Society
350 Fifth Avenue, Suite 801
New York, NY 10118
Tel: 212-308-1414
Email: info@americangeriatrics.org
http://www.americangeriatrics.org

National Gerontological Nursing Association
7794 Grow Drive
Pensacola, FL 32514-7072
Tel: 850-473-1174
Email: ngna@puetzamc.com
http://www.ngna.org

Geriatric Psychiatrists

QUICK FACTS

School Subjects
English
Psychology
Biology

Personal Skills
Helping/teaching
Technical/scientific

Work Environment
Primarily indoors
One location with some
  travel

Minimum Education Level
Medical degree

Salary Range
$120,000 to $163,144 to
  $190,000

Certification or Licensing
Recommended (certification)
Required by all states
  (licensing)

Outlook
About as fast as the average

DOT
070

GOE
02.03.01

NOC
3111

O*NET-SOC
29.1066.00

OVERVIEW

Geriatric psychiatrists are physicians who attend to elderly patients' mental, emotional, and behavioral symptoms. They treat older patients who may suffer from dementia or depression or have other mental illnesses, and they employ different methods to help them function better in their daily lives. For example, geriatric psychiatrists may prescribe medicine, including tranquilizers, antipsychotics, and antidepressants, to help their patients feel better. The medication may also be combined with another therapeutic approach, such as talk therapy. In addition, geriatric psychiatrists may assist nursing-home staff and other caregivers in developing individualized treatment programs and approaches designed to bring improvement to patients.

HISTORY

Although mental illness has been observed and documented for hundreds of years, the major advances in psychiatric treatment came in the latter part of the 19th century. Emil Kraepelin, a German psychiatrist, made an important contribution when he developed a classification system for mental illnesses that is still used for diagnosis. Sigmund Freud, the famous Viennese psychiatrist, developed techniques for analyzing human behavior that have strongly influenced the practice of modern psychiatry.

In the 20th century, the practice of psychiatry underwent another major advancement with the development of medications that could be used in treating psychiatric problems, such as depression and anxiety. Since then, great strides have been made in this area, and medication is very often a component of psychiatric treatment.

The past several decades have seen new challenges emerge in the field, especially in regard to the elderly and their mental health. Medical, industrial, and technological breakthroughs have brought a substantial increase in Americans' life spans; in the 20th century, the average life expectancy increased from approximately 50 years to 75 years. This increase means we have a growing elderly population. The U.S. Census Bureau predicts that the number of Americans age 65 and older will more than double in the first half of the 21st century, increasing from approximately 35 million in 2001 to approximately 82 million in 2050.

Many elderly people in nursing homes and long-term care facilities have a mental illness. Currently, though, most are not getting proper psychiatric treatment; in fact, the vast majority are not receiving

Some Facts from the Alzheimer's Association

Alzheimer's disease causes a person's brain cells to deteriorate and die over the course of several years. The disease is marked by memory loss, dementia, and, eventually, death from loss of brain function. The following are some Alzheimer's statistics from the Alzheimer's Association (http://www.alz.org):

- Approximately 4.5 million Americans have Alzheimer's disease.

- By 2050, 14 million Americans will have Alzheimer's disease unless a cure or prevention is found.

- Ten percent of people over the age of 65 have Alzheimer's disease. Nearly 50 percent of those over age 85 have the disease.

- A small percentage of people get the disease while they are in their 30s or 40s.

- After the onset of symptoms, people with Alzheimer's disease live an average of eight years.

- Seven out of 10 people with Alzheimer's disease live at home and receive most of their care from family or friends. Neither Medicare nor most private health insurance covers the expense of long-term care that most patients need.

- Half of all nursing home residents suffer from Alzheimer's disease or a related disorder.

psychiatric attention at all. Nursing homes were designed to treat people's physical, not mental, problems, and until fairly recently the mental health issues of elderly people were not even recognized by most people, even physicians. Professional recognition for the field of geriatric psychiatry was obtained in 1991 when it was formally recognized as a subspecialty of psychiatry and in 1998 when the American Psychological Association voted to recognize that clinical practice with the elderly requires special training, expertise, and skill.

The growing number of senior citizens in the United States and the proliferation and recognition of Alzheimer's disease, dementia, depression, and other mental diseases and disorders of the elderly point to the need for geriatric psychiatrists.

THE JOB

Geriatric psychiatrists treat elderly patients who suffer from mental and emotional illnesses that make it hard for them to cope with everyday living or to behave in socially acceptable ways. The most common problems treated are dementia and depression, although the elderly can have the same range of disorders as the rest of the population. Often, though, these disorders are not properly diagnosed. According to an article in *Psychiatric News,* experts estimated that one in five seniors has clinically significant anxiety and one in 12 is dependent on alcohol. In addition, these estimates may actually be low since mental illnesses in the elderly are often misdiagnosed or missed altogether.

Geriatric psychiatrists evaluate their patients using a variety of methods, depending on the patient's ability to articulate his or her thoughts and feelings and on the psychiatrist's preferred techniques and practice methods. Geriatric psychiatrists sometimes face special challenges in determining what might be causing erratic or problematic behavior in patients who are unable to express themselves well; sometimes the source of an inappropriate behavior is something relatively simple, such as a urinary tract infection that causes a patient to wet himself or herself. By correctly diagnosing problems, the psychiatrist can not only save the patient distress and discomfort but also avert inappropriate treatments that may be costly and to the patient's detriment.

In other cases, geriatric psychiatrists have to distinguish between the naturally occurring emotional complexities of aging and true illness. Sadness and grief are unquestionably a part of old age. As people reach the last stages of life, they experience many losses, from deterioration of their health and body to deaths of spouses, family members, and friends. The line between this natural sadness and genuine clinical depression can be a thin one. A geriatric psychiatrist must recognize symptoms that point to a genuine depression and treat it accordingly. Just as important, however, the psychiatrist must avoid "medicating away" some of the natural, inescapable feelings that accompany age. Some feelings of sadness may be normal as people realize they have little time left. Part of the geriatric psychiatrist's complex work is to determine what's normal, what's not, and the best course of action in either case.

Because geriatric psychiatrists are medical doctors, they typically begin their patient evaluations with a range of medical tests, including physical and neurological evaluations, laboratory tests, and X rays. These tests will often reveal physical causes for behavioral problems and can result in the psychiatrist referring the patient to a specialist for the needed physical care.

Some psychiatrists rely largely on certain therapeutic techniques in their practices, such as talk therapy or behavior therapy. Naturally, though, these methods are only effective in those willing to try them and grow from the experience. Some people with impairments, such as patients in the late stages of Alzheimer's disease, may not have the ability to process their emotions or communicate clearly. These people may benefit from different therapies. Pharmacotherapy, which is the use of psychotherapeutic medications, such as antidepressants, mood-stabilizing drugs, and tranquilizers, is often used to help elderly patients. Because of this, geriatric psychiatrists must be knowledgeable about potential drug interaction problems, as elderly patients often take a variety of medications for physical problems, such as high cholesterol, arthritis, or diabetes.

No matter what therapy techniques psychiatrists prefer, however, they must individualize treatment programs to meet each patient's needs. Many older people are lonely and simply having someone to talk to on a regular basis can make an extraordinary difference in their attitude and outlook. For other patients, however, talk therapy alone isn't enough to help them feel better, and they benefit from taking medication. The psychiatrist may also use other techniques, such as art therapy (which involves participating in music, dance, or media art), occupational therapy (in which patients learn or relearn skills for caring for themselves), or group therapy (during which a number of patients discuss their personal problems), to help the patient.

Geriatric psychiatrists' practices can take place in several locations. Dr. Michael Pierce, a Connecticut-based geriatric psychiatrist, is in private practice and works as a consultant at a skilled nursing facility two days a week. "In general," he explains, "one has scheduled blocks of times for being at a skilled nursing facility. Other times are spent in the office or in other residential settings, such as assisted living facilities or [senior] day care centers. It's up to the individual's taste what proportion of time is spent in which place."

An unavoidable component of geriatric psychiatrists' job is paperwork. They must do a large amount of documentation, both in keeping patient records up to date and in dealing with Medicare, Medicaid, HMOs, and other insurance companies. More and more psychiatrists, like other health care professionals, are reporting that getting through the increasing amount of red tape and meeting requirements for documentation are encroaching on the time they otherwise would have used to see patients.

Although many geriatric psychiatrists are in private practice, it is likely to become more common for nursing homes and other facilities to employ geriatric psychiatrists full time to better meet the needs of their residents. In this environment, the psychiatrist works as a member of a multidisciplinary team, including other nursing home staff. The team shares information, develops appropriate therapeutic approaches, and monitors the treatment for each patient. Because the number of elderly people in our country is large and growing rapidly, geriatric psychiatrists should have many opportunities. Nursing homes and other care facilities that have geriatric psychiatrists on staff will be seen by seniors and their families as institutions that offer quality care.

REQUIREMENTS

High School

If you think medical school is in your future, you should focus on college preparatory classes in high school. Take plenty of science and math courses, including biology, chemistry, physics, algebra, and calculus. To prepare for your later psychology studies, take sociology, psychology, and history classes. English courses that teach you to research, write, and speak well are also important, as you will need to express yourself clearly not only to patients but also to the other professionals you'll be working with. Dr. Michael Pierce recommends taking a well-rounded curriculum. "I wish I had taken more art and literature, philosophy, business, political science, and so forth. In other words, take whatever courses interest you."

Postsecondary Training

Since you will need to attend medical school to become a geriatric psychiatrist, you should plan your college curriculum to meet medical school admission requirements. You will benefit from consulting the Association of American Medical Colleges' annual publication *Medical School Admission Requirements, United States and Canada,* which has information on schools' entrance requirements, as well as information on other topics such as schools' curricula and financial aid. Typical majors for those planning on attending medical school include biology, chemistry, and biochemistry. You should also continue to take psychology and English classes. Some universities now offer undergraduate courses in gerontology that cover topics such as the sociology of aging and public policy issues affecting the elderly. Scores from the Medical College Admission Test are required for admission by most medical schools. Students usually take this test during their junior year of college.

In medical school, you will need to complete a four-year program of medical studies and supervised clinical work to earn your M.D. degree. Most instruction in the first two years is given through classroom lectures, laboratories, seminars, and the reading of textbook material. You will also learn to take medical histories, examine patients, and recognize symptoms.

During the last two years of medical school, you will become actively involved in the treatment process, spending a large proportion of your time in the hospital as part of a medical team headed by a teaching physician. You will be closely supervised as you learn techniques such as how to take a patient's medical history, how to make a physical examination, how to work in the laboratory, how to make a diagnosis, and how to keep all the necessary records. In addition to this hospital work, you will continue to take course work.

Once you have completed four years of medical school, you will need to complete a residency. First-year residents work in several specialties, such as pediatrics or internal medicine. After that, residents wanting to become psychiatrists complete three years of work at a psychiatric hospital or a general hospital's psychiatric ward. In addition, residents may complete a geriatric psychiatry fellowship, a program typically lasting one year and providing specialized geriatric training. Completing such a fellowship is highly recommended.

Certification or Licensing

The American Board of Psychiatry and Neurology (ABPN) is the certifying board for all psychiatrists regardless of their specialty. To become an ABPN-certified psychiatrist you will need to pass a written and an oral test. An ABPN-certified psychiatrist may treat geriatric patients. Those in the field, however, recommend that you complete a geriatric psychiatry fellowship program, which qualifies you to apply for the subspecialty certification of geriatric psychiatrist. To obtain this subspecialty certification, also available through ABPN, you must pass a written exam covering topics such as psychological and social aspects of aging and diagnostic methods. This certification is highly recommended because it will enhance your professional standing as well as demonstrate to your patients and their families your extensive training in this field.

After receiving their M.D. degree, all doctors must pass a licensing test in order to practice medicine in the state in which they will work. Depending on the requirements of your state, you may need to pass the National Board of Medical Examiners test, the Federal Licensing Examination, or an individual state licensing test. Because these requirements vary, you will need to check with your state's licensing board for specific information.

Other Requirements

Geriatric psychiatrists need to be compassionate, patient, flexible, and intelligent. To be effective in their work, they must understand a vast array of medical, technical, and psychological information. They need analyzing and diagnosing skills, excellent listening skills, and administrative skills. Decision-making ability, time-management skills, and writing skills are also important in this career. Like any doctor, they must be committed to lifelong learning in order to keep up with advancements in the field, such as new medications.

Perhaps most important, though, geriatric psychiatrists must enjoy working with older people, listening to them and helping them with their unique set of problems. A successful geriatric psychiatrist must have a firm belief that, with the right treatment, mentally ill seniors can get relief from their pain and lead improved and fulfilling lives.

EXPLORING

You should take advantage of any available opportunities to learn more about the psychiatric field and about working with the elderly. Use your local library or a computer with an Internet connection as resources to literature on the field. You can learn about psychotherapy in general by reading books such as *Inside Therapy: Illuminating Writings about Therapists, Patients, and Psychotherapy* (Ilana Rabinowitz, ed., New York: Griffin Trade Paperback, 2000). You can also take a look at articles from the *American Journal of Geriatric Psychiatry,* which is the official publication for the American Association for Geriatric Psychiatry. Articles from the journal are available online at http://ajgp.psychiatryonline.org. You can also ask your high school guidance counselor for help in setting up an informational interview with a local psychiatrist or other physician. Even if you are only able to talk to a family doctor, you can still ask him or her what medical school was like, what college courses were particularly helpful to take, and other general questions about the profession.

It is very important that you get experience working with the elderly. Hands-on experience will allow you to find out how much you like working with this group of people, and it will make you a more desirable candidate when you apply to colleges and medical schools. Begin in high school by getting a summer or part-time job at a hospital, clinic, senior day program, or nursing home. Dr. Michael Pierce recommends that high school students seek jobs as certified nursing assistants, which would provide hands-on experience taking care of geriatric patients. If you are unable to find paid work, become a volunteer.

EMPLOYERS

Approximately half of all practicing psychiatrists work in private practice; many others combine private practice with work in a health care institution. These institutions include private hospitals, state mental hospitals, medical schools, community health centers, and government health agencies. Psychiatrists also work for health maintenance organizations and in nursing homes. They are employed throughout the country.

While it is still most common for geriatric psychiatrists to work either alone or as part of a group in private practice, there will likely be a growing trend for skilled nursing facilities to employ full-time psychiatrists. This serves to improve care to residents because the psychiatrist is able to form ongoing relationships with the patients as well as ongoing relationships with the staff. In addition, the psychiatrist can work closely with the staff on treatment plans and give advice or instruction on how to deal with the various challenges facing the patients. Currently more than 2,300 board-certified geriatric psychiatrists work in the United States.

STARTING OUT

Professional journals and organizations, such as the American Psychiatric Association and the American Association for Geriatric Psychiatry, can provide good job leads for beginning geriatric psychiatrists. Many doctors are offered permanent positions with the same institution where their residency was completed. Those new psy-chiatrists who choose to specialize in geriatrics may have an advan-tage because the rapidly increasing numbers of elderly people means a growing client base. In nursing homes and in general, this popula-tion is underserved and in particular need of access to psychiatric services.

ADVANCEMENT

In geriatric psychiatry as well as other physician specialties, advance-ment usually comes in the form of an increased clientele and increased earnings that result from the psychiatrist's good reputation, skills, and up-to-date knowledge. Those who work in hospitals, clinics, and mental health centers may choose to advance by becoming adminis-trators. Other geriatric psychiatrists may be drawn to research and academia, where they may advance to become department heads.

EARNINGS

Like other physicians, psychiatrists' average income is among the highest of all professionals. Psychiatrists' earnings are determined by their experience, number of patients, location, and type of practice. As Dr. Michael Pierce points out, "The physicians who make the most money are not necessarily the best clinicians. Many have elaborated an efficient 'system' that maximizes compensation per time spent without necessarily maximizing quality care. Good care is time con-suming, and Medicare pays only 40 percent . . . or less of the usual fee that can be earned in a general office practice."

Physicians Search, a placement service for doctors, also conduct-ed a salary survey in 2001. According to this survey, psychiatrists reported incomes ranging from $120,000 to $139,000. The Medical Group Management Association's *Physician Compensation and Management Report, 2003* reports that psychiatrists make an aver-age of $163,144 a year, which includes base salary, bonuses, research stipends, etc. Self-employed physicians generally have higher incomes than salaried physicians, sometimes making more than $190,000 a year, but they must also provide their own benefits.

As to geriatric psychiatrists employed by nursing homes, the newsletter *Psychiatric Times* notes that some geriatric psychiatrists report salary offers of $140,000 a year. In addition, those who work for nursing homes usually receive benefits, such as health insurance and retirement plans, that doctors with their own practices must provide for themselves.

WORK ENVIRONMENT

Geriatric psychiatrists in private practice set their own schedules and usually work regular hours. While other kinds of psychiatrists are likely to work some evenings or weekends to accommodate patients who work, geriatric psychiatrists' patients typically have fairly open daytime schedules. Some geriatric psychiatrists work as few as 35–40 hours a week; others might work as many as 70. This depends on the type of practice, the size of the clientele, and the personal goals and desires of the psychiatrist. Geriatric psychiatrists, like other kinds of psychiatrists, may spend a certain amount of time on call. This means they need to be accessible to their patients and available to handle or advise on any crisis that might arise.

Geriatric psychiatrists in private practice typically work in comfortable office settings. Other settings may vary; consulting work in nursing homes might be somewhat less comfortable, both because the environment can be disturbing or depressing at times and because the psychiatrist may not have a designated work area. Because many geriatric psychiatrists work in a consultant capacity to various nursing or day facilities, they are more likely than other psychiatrists and physicians to commute with some frequency and work in multiple locations.

OUTLOOK

Job opportunities for physicians in general are expected to grow about as fast as the average through 2012, according to the Department of Labor. Opportunities for geriatric psychiatrists both in private practice and in salaried positions are excellent. The demand for psychiatrists serving seniors is high, and the demand is growing each year as this population increases. A recent article in *Psychiatric News* reports that Dr. Soo Borson, president of the American Association for Geriatric Psychiatry, predicted mental disorders in people over the age of 65 to increase by 275 percent by the year 2030.

As the importance of mental health care for our elderly is increasingly recognized and accepted, it should become easier for seniors and their families to have access to and support in securing treatment. One concern that may limit the number of elderly seeking mental health care is financial. Medicare payments for psychiatric treatments are very limited, and as Dr. Michael Pierce points out, good care is expensive. Government health care reforms, however, may make mental health care available to more people.

In addition to the need for geriatric psychiatrists to work in clinical practice (seeing patients), there is a strong need for geriatric psychiatrists to work in research and academia. Overall, employment in this field should grow at a good rate.

FOR MORE INFORMATION

For resources aimed at older people, their families, and their caregivers, check out the following website:
Administration on Aging
Washington, DC 20201
Tel: 202-619-7501
Email: aoainfo@aoa.gov
http://www.aoa.gov

For information about Alzheimer's disease, caregiving, and local chapters of the association, contact
Alzheimer's Association
225 North Michigan Avenue, Floor 17
Chicago, IL 60611-1676
Tel: 800-272-3900
Email: info@alz.org
http://www.alz.org

For information on aging and mental health from a medical perspective, contact
American Association for Geriatric Psychiatry
7910 Woodmont Avenue, Suit 1050
Bethesda, MD 20814-3004
Tel: 301-654-7850
Email: main@aagponline.org
http://www.aagpgpa.org

For information on choosing a medical specialty, as well as a description of psychiatry, contact
American Medical Association
515 North State Street
Chicago, IL 60610
Tel: 800-621-8335
http://www.ama-assn.org

For brochures of general information, contact
American Psychiatric Association
1000 Wilson Boulevard, Suit 1825
Arlington, VA 22209
Tel: 703-907-7300
Email: apa@psych.org
http://www.psych.org

For more information on choosing a medical school, the application process, and careers in medicine, contact
Association of American Medical Colleges
2450 N Street, NW
Washington, DC 20037-1126
Tel: 202-828-0400
http://www.aamc.org

For information on improving the health and well being of older Americans through research, contact
National Institute on Aging
Building 31, Room 5C27
31 Center Drive, MSC 2292
Bethesda, MD 20892
Tel: 301-496-1752
http://www.nih.gov/nia

For information on mental illness, contact
National Mental Health Association
2001 North Beauregard Street, 12th Floor
Alexandria, VA 22311
Tel: 800-969-6642
Email: infoctr@nmha.org
http://www.nmha.org

For information about the practice of psychiatry in Canada, contact
Canadian Psychiatric Association
260-441 MacLaren Street
Ottawa, ON K2P-2H3
Canada
Tel: 613-234-2815
Email: cpa@cpa-apc.org
http://www.cpa-apc.org

Geriatric Social Workers

QUICK FACTS

School Subjects
Psychology
Sociology

Personal Skills
Helping/teaching
Leadership/management

Work Environment
Primarily indoors
Primarily multiple locations

Minimum Education Level
Bachelor's degree

Salary Range
$23,840 to $37,380 to
$56,320

Certification or Licensing
Recommended (certification)
Required by all states
(licensing)

Outlook
Faster than the average

DOT
195

GOE
10.01.02

NOC
4152

O*NET-SOC
21-1021.00, 21-1022.00,
21-1023.00

OVERVIEW

Geriatric social workers, also known as *gerontology social workers,* help elderly people adjust to the challenges of growing older. They develop programs and direct agencies that offer counseling, advocacy, and special services. They evaluate the needs of clients and help them arrange for such things as meal service, housing, transportation, and legal and medical assistance. Geriatric social workers also develop recreation and educational programs for the elderly.

Approximately one-third of all social workers work with older people. They work in hospitals, nursing homes, and retirement communities; they have offices in human service agencies and senior centers. Geriatric social workers must have a genuine interest in the well-being of older people and must be sensitive to their concerns and problems.

HISTORY

Social workers were often the villains of old movies. They were often portrayed as either stiff, unemotional women carrying briefcases and wearing long dark skirts, or as thin, bald men with beady eyes behind thick glasses. With little emotion, they dragged children off to orphanages, committed sane people to insane asylums, and threatened the poor and elderly. The goal of the social worker seemed to be to uphold social norms by breaking up unconventional families. This may reflect a moral superiority that tainted social work up until the early 20th century. Today, the social services industry is responsible for empowering individuals (such as the poor, elderly, and ill) and helping them to face personal problems and address large social issues.

Theories and methodologies of social work have changed over the years, but the basis of the profession has remained the same: helping people address hardships such as poverty, illness, drug addictions, and aging. As society changes, so do its problems, calling for redefinition of the social work profession. The U.S. population is getting older. According to the National Association of Social Workers, individuals over the age of 65 now outnumber teenagers. Changing demographics have created a need for experienced professionals in geriatrics. Geriatric social workers help older individuals and their families to cope with the difficulties encountered in aging, such as maintaining mental and physical health and overcoming feelings of depression or fears of dying.

THE JOB

A woman in her late 70s has just lost her husband and now must live alone for the first time in many years. She has decided to move to another town to live closer to her children and will need help making the transition. She needs a smaller, more manageable home; she needs help with meals and shopping; she would like to make friends in the community. A number of services are available to her, but she may not find out about them without the aid of a geriatric social worker.

As with any social worker, the geriatric social worker is devoted to helping people and communities solve problems. Social workers are dedicated to empowering people and helping people to preserve their dignity and feeling of worth. This kind of assistance and advocacy is especially important among older people. Because old age can sometimes put a person in poor physical and mental health as well as cause financial difficulties, older people often need help and protection. They may need help with preparing meals, finding transportation, and doing housework, or they may need assistance moving into a retirement community or nursing home. But the elderly population of any community is diverse; some older people stay in perfectly good health, and they rely on social services for recreation, meeting people, educational programs, and grief and loss counseling.

People are living longer these days, and the elderly population is growing. At the beginning of the 20th century, only one-half of newborns would live past the age of 50; people born at the beginning of the 21st century can, on average, expect to live well past the age of 75. This is why social work will continue to offer many job opportunities.

The social work profession is divided into two areas: direct practice and indirect practice. Direct practice is also known as clinical practice. As the name suggests, direct practice involves working directly with the client by offering counseling, advocacy, information and referral, and education. Indirect practice (a practice consisting mostly of social workers who hold Ph.D.'s) concerns the structures through which the direct practice is offered. Indirect practice involves program development and evaluation, administration, and policy analysis. Geriatric social workers may work directly with the elderly population through counseling, advising, and conducting group sessions. They also help clients find services for health, housing, finances, and transportation. Those social workers involved in indirect practice develop and oversee the agencies and departments that provide these social services.

Geriatric social workers work for service agencies, hospitals, nursing homes, senior centers, and other community organizations. Some also work independently. Their help is needed in every town and city across the country; some social workers in areas with smaller populations may serve a number of small towns within a region. No matter where a geriatric social worker serves, the nature of the work is usually the same. Geriatric social workers meet with older people individually to determine their needs. Home meal delivery programs, transportation services, and recreational programs are some of the basic services offered by community organizations. Some organizations also offer home health care. With nurses and aides assigned to visit the elderly in their homes and to help them with their housework and medical needs, elderly clients can continue to live on their own.

Geriatric social workers evaluate clients by interviewing them and determining their needs; social workers then enroll clients for these services. They make phone calls and provide the service agencies with client information.

The client may need even more assistance. Adult day care services are available in some cities, as are adult foster care services that match older people with families. A social worker may also need to help a client arrange to move into a nursing home and counsel the client about the transition. These counseling services are also extended to members of the client's family, advising them in how to deal with a parent's or grandparent's aging or illness.

In some cases, an elderly person is neglected or taken advantage of. A geriatric social worker can look into these cases and serve as an advocate, stepping in to advise the client of his or her legal rights. In addition to legal services, a geriatric social worker will help a client locate any needed financial services. Social workers help clients make arrangements for the payment of services through Medicare and other financial aid.

Because of efforts by the government to improve the quality of nursing home care, social workers are becoming more active within these facilities. These geriatric social workers work closely with the elderly and their families in arranging the move into the nursing home. They also counsel families upon the death of an elderly relative and help with funeral arrangements. Geriatric social workers also protect and promote the rights of the residents, and they may train nursing care staff members on patient rights.

The geriatric social worker is part of the larger field of aging. This field, which works to provide help for older people while researching the process of aging, is composed of hospitals, health care corporations, government agencies, churches, colleges, and other organizations and institutions. Various professions, such as law, psychology, health care, education, and marketing, include specialties in aging, or gerontology.

REQUIREMENTS

High School
Since you will need at least a bachelor's degree to advance in this field, prepare by taking a college prep curriculum in high school. This should include math, science, and computer science classes. Other courses that will help you in this field include civics or government courses, in which you can learn about the enactment of laws, such as the Older Americans Act. Psychology and sociology courses will help you gain an understanding of human behavior and the process of aging as well as teach you methods for studying groups of people, such as the elderly. Take English classes to develop your writing, speaking, and researching skills—skills that you will need throughout your career.

Postsecondary Training
Although you may be able to work in some levels of geriatric social work with only a high school diploma or associate's degree, most professional opportunities exist for people with bachelor's or more advanced degrees in social work. The Council on Social Work Education, which accredits bachelor's and master's programs in social work, has approved 436 programs granting the bachelor's degree in social work (B.S.W.) and 149 programs granting the master's degree (M.S.W.). The council offers the *Directory of Colleges and*

Universities with Accredited Social Work Degree Programs, providing contact information. In addition, the council's website (http://www.cswe.org) has a member program directory that lists accredited programs by state. The Group for the Advancement of Doctoral Education provides contact information for 78 programs that offer the doctor of social work (D.S.W.) degree or the Ph.D. in social work (visit the website at http://www.socwk.utah.edu/gade/index.html). Accredited B.S.W. programs include courses in human behavior and the social environment, social welfare policy and services, social work practice, research, and field practicum. Most programs require two years of liberal arts study, followed by two years of study in the social work major. Students must also complete a field practicum of at least 400 hours.

Although no clear lines of classification are drawn in the social work profession, most supervisory and administrative positions require at least a master's degree in social work. Master's programs are organized according to fields of practice (such as mental health care), problem areas (substance abuse), population groups (the elderly), and practice roles (practice with individuals, families, or communities). They are usually two-year programs, requiring at least 900 hours of field practice.

Doctoral degrees are usually necessary for research and teaching. Many social workers with doctorates work in community organizations.

Certification or Licensing

The practice of social work is regulated in all states and the District of Columbia. To receive the necessary licensing, a social worker typically has to gain a certain amount of experience and pass an exam. Because requirements vary by state, you will need to check with the regulatory board in your state for specific information. Licensing information is also available from the Association of Social Work Boards (http://www.aswb.org).

The National Association of Social Workers (NASW) offers certification in several areas. All social workers who meet requirements, which include education, experience, and passing an exam, may receive the designation Academy of Certified Social Workers. In addition, NASW offers specialty certifications, and certification as a qualified clincial social worker and as a diplomate in clinical social work to those who meet specific education, practice, and other requirements. Although certification is voluntary, it is highly recommended for anyone wanting to advance in the field. Certification demonstrates that you have gained the knowledge and experience necessary to meet national standards.

Other Requirements

To be a successful geriatric social worker, you must care about the needs and problems of older people. Many of these people will be relying on you to help them through crucial and difficult times; you must be completely dedicated to your clients and devoted to helping them maintain their dignity and sense of self-worth.

Most geriatric social workers are involved directly with the people they serve, and they are expected to carefully examine a client's living habits and family relations. A geriatric social worker has to be prepared to confront depressing situations occasionally. In most cases, though, a good geriatric social worker will take pleasure from helping a client through a rough time and will take pride in seeing the client improve his or her life. It is also important for a geriatric social worker to be good-natured and friendly; clients resistant to change may refuse to cooperate with someone they find unpleasant. A geriatric social worker must be very sensitive to the problems of the elderly but must also remain supportive and encouraging.

EXPLORING

Volunteering is one of the best ways to explore your interest in geriatric social work. Check with nursing homes, senior care centers, or organizations such as Meals on Wheels in your area for volunteer opportunities. Another way to gain experience is to get summer or part-time work at a local hospital, nursing home, or home health care agency. Home health care aides have the opportunity to work closely with the elderly and to get to know their needs and concerns. Also, as a college student enrolled in a social work program, you may have the opportunity to help a faculty member with a gerontological research project.

EMPLOYERS

Opportunities for geriatric social workers can be found in both the public and private sectors. Hospitals, nursing homes, retirement communities, human services offices, senior centers, and government agencies all employ geriatric social workers. With so many services available for older people, there are a variety of job opportunities for the geriatric social worker. There are some agencies that deal only with the practical aspects of aiding older people, such as arranging for services and managing financial and legal issues. Working for other agencies may involve the organization of recreational and educational activities, such as senior theater groups and art classes.

STARTING OUT

After receiving your social work degree and gaining some field experience, you will have made valuable connections among faculty and social service organizations. These connections may be able to help you find a job. Your college's job-placement service or internship program may also direct you to your first full-time position. You should also become familiar with the local senior centers and agencies for the elderly.

Joining a professional organization can be helpful in entering the field. The American Society on Aging sponsors a job bank and publishes newsletters. Job opportunities are listed in the newsletters of the American Geriatrics Society, the American Counseling Association, and other professional organizations. You should also attend annual meetings, which give you the chance to meet other people working in social work, geriatrics, and gerontology.

ADVANCEMENT

Most geriatric social workers enter the field focusing on the work rather than on the promotions and salary raises. However, there are advancement opportunities for dedicated social workers. Successful social workers may move up the ranks of their organizations to become supervisors or directors, taking on additional responsibilities such as overseeing new hires. A key factor in achieving the most advanced positions is to have advanced education. Those who move into the higher paid positions in administration, program development, or policy analysis must have a Ph.D. or, in some cases, a master's degree with practical experience.

Within smaller agencies and in smaller towns, advancement opportunities may be few, but there may also be less competition for these jobs. A greater number of advancement opportunities may be available in service organizations in urban areas.

EARNINGS

The Department of Labor reports that the median annual earnings of medical and public health social workers, a group that includes geriatric social workers, were $37,380 in 2002. The lowest paid 10 percent made less than $23,840, and the highest paid 10 percent made more than $56,320. Geriatric social workers working in nursing care facilities made median annual salaries of $33,330.

Median annual earnings for substance abuse and mental health social workers, a category that also includes geriatric social workers, were $32,850 in 2002. Those working for state governments made $38,430 a year, and those working for local governments made $35,700.

Social workers' benefits depend on the employer, but they generally include health insurance and paid vacation time.

WORK ENVIRONMENT

Although geriatric social workers do spend some time in an office setting, they spend much of their time interviewing clients and the directors of programs; they also visit the homes of their clients to evaluate and take notes. They may also visit the homes of clients' families. Although some geriatric social workers may work in hospital and nursing home environments, others have their offices in human service agencies alongside other service providers. Serving as an advocate for the elderly client requires, in addition to phone calls and faxes, personal meetings with directors of agencies, local legislators, and others. In cases of abuse and neglect, it may require testifying in court.

Because poverty and illness afflict a large number of people over the age of 65, the geriatric social worker is often assigned depressing, seemingly hopeless cases. This may be the situation only temporarily, however, as the social worker introduces the client to the necessary services and assistance.

OUTLOOK

The field of social work is expected to grow faster than the average through 2012, according to the U.S. Department of Labor. Those specializing in geriatric social work in particular will be in great demand for several reasons. It is estimated that as people live longer—more than 15 million people in the United States will be over the age of 85 by the middle of the 21st century—more geriatric social workers will be needed to create programs and provide services for the growing number of elderly persons. Rising health care costs are causing many insurance companies to consider alternatives to hospital treatment, so some insurance coverage now includes home stays. In addition, hospitals and nursing homes are trying to balance the demand for their services and their limitations in staff and physical facilities. As home care becomes a viable, affordable option for more older people, more geriatric social workers will be necessary to evaluate the needs of clients and set up services.

The Omnibus Budget Reconciliation Act (OBRA) passed by the U.S. Congress in 1987 to improve nursing home care requires large nursing care facilities to employ full-time social workers. As the government becomes more involved in providing better care for the elderly, the geriatric social worker will see more full-time job opportunities in nursing homes and hospitals.

FOR MORE INFORMATION

To read Careers in Aging, *visit the following website:*
Association for Gerontology in Higher Education
1030 15th Street, NW, Suite 240
Washington, DC 20005-1503
Tel: 202-289-9806
Email: info@aghe.org
http://www.aghe.org

For information on licensing, contact
Association of Social Work Boards
400 South Ridge Parkway, Suite B
Culpeper, VA 22701
Tel: 800-225-6880
Email: info@aswb.org
http://www.aswb.org

For information on education and the field of social work, contact
Council on Social Work Education
1725 Duke Street, Suite 500
Alexandria, VA 22314-3457
Tel: 703-683-8080
Email: info@cswe.org
http://www.cswe.org

For certification information and to read Choices: Careers in Social Work, *visit the following website:*
National Association of Social Workers
750 First Street, NE, Suite 700
Washington, DC 20002-4241
Tel: 202-408-8600
Email: info@naswdc.org
http://www.naswdc.org

For more information on careers in geriatric social work, contact the following organizations:

American Association of Homes and Services for the Aging
2519 Connecticut Avenue, NW
Washington, DC 20008-1520
Tel: 202-783-2242
Email: info@aahsa.org
http://www.aahsa.org

American Geriatrics Society
350 Fifth Avenue, Suite 801
New York, NY 10118
Tel: 212-308-1414
Email: info@americangeriatrics.org
http://www.americangeriatrics.org

American Society on Aging
833 Market Street, Suite 511
San Francisco, CA 94103-1824
Tel: 800-537-9728
Email: info@asaging.org
http://www.asaging.org

Gerontological Society of America
1030 15th Street, NW, Suite 250
Washington, DC 20005
Tel: 202-842-1275
Email: geron@geron.org
http://www.geron.org

National Association of Area Agencies on Aging
1730 Rhode Island Avenue, NW, Suite 1200
Washington, DC 20036
Tel: 202-872-0888
http://www.n4a.org

Grief Therapists

School Subjects
Psychology
Sociology

Personal Skills
Communication/ideas
Helping/teaching

Work Environment
Primarily indoors
Primarily one location

Minimum Education Level
Master's degree

Salary Range
$19,760 to $29,940 to
$50,170+

Certification or Licensing
Voluntary (certification)
Required by certain states
(licensing)

Outlook
Faster than the average

DOT
195

GOE
10.01.02

NOC
4153

O*NET-SOC
19-3031.03

OVERVIEW

A *grief therapist* or *bereavement counselor* offers therapy for those who are mourning the death of a family member or a loved one. Therapists help survivors work through possible feelings of anger or guilt and help them recover from their loss. Counselors may be brought into communities or facilities to help individuals after a national disaster, act of violence, or an accident. Grief therapists may be self-employed as independent counselors or work for hospitals, funeral homes, schools, hospice organizations, nursing homes, or government or private agencies.

HISTORY

Grief therapy is a relatively new career specialty. According to Dr. Dana Cable, professor of psychology at Hood College in Frederick, Maryland, and a certified grief therapist, "Grief therapy is a growing area because of the nature of many deaths today. There are many more issues to be worked through when we lose young people to violent deaths and diseases such as AIDS. In addition, there is some movement away from organized religion where people used to find comfort when they lost a loved one." Cable also points out that changes in the family unit have affected the way in which family members grieve. Many families are not close, physically or emotionally, resulting in issues of guilt when a family member dies. Other factors that have boosted growth in this field include people's willingness to accept the help of a therapist (something that rarely happened in years past) and the large number of aging baby boomers who are now beginning to experience the deaths of friends and family members and, thus, have a need for grief therapists' services.

THE JOB

Grief therapists help individuals accept the death of a spouse, child, partner, parent, sibling, or loved one. Therapists give their clients reassurance and help them examine and resolve feelings, including negative ones, that may be associated with the death. Counseling may be done on a one-to-one basis, with a small group, or as part of a support group.

When disasters such as accidents or violence occur, grief therapists are often brought in to speak to communities, schools, or organizations. They help people deal with the tragedy and may provide individual counseling. In recent times, therapists have been called upon when violence has hit schools, when weather-related tragedies have destroyed communities, and when an airplane has crashed or terrorist bombing has occurred.

Hospitals, nursing homes, AIDS and cancer care centers, and hospice organizations employ grief therapists to provide emotional support to patients and their families and friends. In addition, some funeral homes refer families and friends to grief therapists as part of an aftercare service following a funeral.

Grief therapists also work as *death educators*. These specialists conduct classes for people who work in professions that deal with the sick and dying, such as medical and nursing students. They may also speak to organizations, clubs, support groups, parents, and others about issues related to death and give them suggestions on how to cope.

REQUIREMENTS

High School

College prep classes are essential if you wish to enter the field of grief therapy. In order to learn how to deal with a diverse group of people from all cultural backgrounds, courses in health, sociology, psychology, and religion are helpful. Communication is a key part of the grief therapist's job, so speech, foreign languages, communication, and English courses are also vital. It may be a good idea to check with the colleges you have selected to find out what courses they recommend for a career in psychology and counseling.

Postsecondary Training

Degrees that are strong in psychology or a premed program are usually recommended for counselors. This must be followed with a master's program in counseling, social work, or psychology. Following this with a doctoral degree in psychology is recommended for the best job prospects.

Certification and Licensing

The Association for Death Education and Counseling offers the certified in thanatology: death, dying and bereavement (CT) designation. Candidates must complete educational and work requirements and pass an examination in order to receive this voluntary certification.

The National Board for Certified Counselors Inc. (NBCC) offers the national certified counselor credential. Candidates must have at least a master's degree in counseling from an accredited college or university, two years of experience, and pass an examination administered by the NBCC.

Some states require grief therapists to obtain licenses in order to practice. These licensing requirements may vary from state to state, so it is best to check with the state in which you plan to practice. Some states may limit counselors' private practices to areas in which they have developed professional competence. There may also be some continuing education requirements for license renewal.

Other Requirements

If you are interested in becoming a grief therapist, you should enjoy working with people and feel comfortable dealing with the sick and dying. You should show patience and be a compassionate listener, as well as be able to express yourself clearly and tactfully.

Grief therapists must not let their jobs take an emotional toll on their own lives. Though they hear many stories of grief and sadness, therapists can also find their job rewarding and uplifting as they help people overcome feelings of depression and despair and continue on with their lives.

EXPLORING

Your high school guidance counselor may be able to supply information on a career as a therapist. Other sources for information can be found at your local or school library, or through the Internet. Contact the organizations listed at the end of this article for further information.

Doing volunteer work for organizations such as the Red Cross or with your local hospital, nursing home, or hospice care center will give you more experience dealing with the sick, troubled, or grieving. Participating in high school clubs or other groups that organize volunteer projects to benefit homeless people, victims of AIDS, or battered spouses can also give you valuable experience.

EMPLOYERS

Grief therapists may provide grief therapy as an independent part of their larger counseling practice, or they may work as part of an organization. Many therapists in private practice offer grief therapy. Some therapists are part of a group practice of medical or psychological professionals who offer a variety of counseling and therapy services. Funeral homes, nursing homes, assisted care facilities, AIDS care facilities, hospice organizations, and almost any facility or organization that deals with the sick and dying use grief therapists. Many have a therapist either on call or on staff. The government may also employ counselors and grief therapists in their health care facilities.

Some grief therapists may work under contract with large corporations as part of employee assistance programs. Others may be called upon by airlines, schools, communities, or businesses at times of crisis or when violence has occurred. They may also work on a contract basis to make presentations or seminars to various groups or organizations.

Grief therapists may also work at colleges or universities, conducting research or teaching classes that deal with death and grief.

STARTING OUT

Some colleges and universities offer job placement for people seeking careers in counseling. While in graduate school, therapy students often work as interns with hospitals, hospices, health care, or crisis care organizations, or with therapists in private practices. These relationships can often offer employment and networking possibilities after graduation.

Most grief therapists practice general counseling before specializing in grief therapy. Building a client base as a counselor can help provide the base for beginning a career in grief therapy. Personal contacts can also provide networking possibilities. Membership in a professional counseling association may offer sources for contacts and help you find job leads. Classified advertisements and trade magazines also list job openings.

ADVANCEMENT

Counselors specializing in grief therapy can advance to head their own counseling service or group practice, serving clients directly or contracting out services to hospitals, businesses, hospice organizations, and other facilities. Experienced grief therapists who specialize in education can become department heads of universities or colleges. Counselors with a business background and experience can advance to become executive directors of health care facilities, organizations, nursing homes, or head professional organizations that serve the counseling profession.

EARNINGS

The salary range for grief therapists is generally the same as for other therapists and counselors. According to the U.S. Department of Labor, the median annual salary of mental health counselors was $29,940 in 2002. The lowest 10 percent earned less than $19,760, and the highest 10 percent earned more than $50,170. Therapists in private practice and those who become directors of facilities may earn considerably more.

Benefits vary depending on the position and the employer but generally vacation, sick leave, insurance, and other work-related bene-

Where You Might Find a Grief Therapist at Work

- Private practice
- Day care centers
- Schools
- Colleges
- Churches
- Corporations
- Businesses
- Hospice agencies
- Nursing homes
- Assisted living homes
- Sites of accidents or natural disasters
- Hospitals
- Trauma centers
- Cancer care centers
- AIDS treatment centers
- Industrial accident sites
- Funeral homes
- Armed forces

fits are provided. Persons who are self-employed usually have to provide their own insurance and retirement funds.

WORK ENVIRONMENT

Generally, grief therapists work in office settings that are clean and
well lighted. Grief therapists who work in crisis situations will find
a wide variety of working environments depending on the situation,
but usually small, temporary offices are set up to accommodate counselors.

Counselors in private or group practice may have to set up evening
and weekend office hours. Some grief counseling must be done on an
emergency basis in times of crisis or violence, so there may be occa-
sions when counselors have to drop everything to work any time of
the day or night.

Many counselors stick to a given location to serve the local community. However, depending on the type and range of cases the therapist handles, travel may be necessary, including on nights and
weekends.

OUTLOOK

According to the *Occupational Outlook Handbook,* employment
opportunities in the counseling field are expected to grow faster than
the average for all occupations through 2012. Demand should be
strongest for counselors concentrating on rehabilitation and on mental health, which includes grief therapy.

A career in grief therapy holds great promise. Our changing
and aging society creates a need for grief counseling. As baby
boomers age and experience the deaths of their parents, friends,
and families, they are seeking the help of bereavement counselors
to help them adjust and deal with their feelings. Counseling has
become a socially accepted tool to help people deal with difficult
or painful situations.

As violent crimes occur and as young people witness acts of violence and experience the untimely death of friends, they seek an
understanding that grief counselors can help provide. Car accidents,
AIDS, and drug-related deaths can also create feelings of guilt and
depression that counselors can help people work through.
Unfortunately, there will continue to be natural disasters such as tor-
nadoes, floods, avalanches, and earthquakes that kill large numbers
of people. Grief counselors will continue to be called on to help ease
survivors' pain.

Although grief therapists work in every part of the country, demand is highest in retirement areas of the country where there is a large elderly population.

FOR MORE INFORMATION

For career and certification information, contact the following organizations:

American Counseling Association
5999 Stevenson Avenue
Alexandria, VA 22304
Tel: 800-347-6647
http://www.counseling.org

Association for Death Education and Counseling
342 North Main Street
West Hartford, CT 06117-2507
Tel: 860-586-7503
Email: info@adec.org
http://www.adec.org

For information on working with grieving children and their families, contact

Dougy Center
National Center for Grieving Children and Families
PO Box 86852
Portland, OR 97286
Tel: 503-775-5683
Email: help@dougy.org
http://www.grievingchild.org

For information on working with the elderly, contact

Gerontological Society of America
1030 15th Street, NW, Suite 250
Washington, DC 20005
Tel: 202-842-1275
Email: geron@geron.org
http://www.geron.org

For information on graduate programs in thanatology, or the study of grief therapy, contact the following colleges:

College of New Rochelle
Graduate School, Division of Human Services
29 Castle Place
New Rochelle, NY 10805
Tel: 914-654-5561
Email: gs@cnr.edu
http://cnr.edu

Hood College
401 Rosemont Avenue
Frederick, MD 21701-8575
Tel: 301-663-3131
Email: hoodgrad@hood.edu
http://www.hood.edu

Health Advocates

OVERVIEW

Health advocates, also known as *patient representatives* and *patient advocates,* work with and on behalf of patients to resolve issues ranging from getting insurance coverage to dealing with complaints about the medical staff to explaining a doctor's treatment plan. In addition to patients, health advocates often deal with physicians, hospitals, health maintenance organizations, insurance companies, and government agencies, to name a few. Advocates are employed by hospitals, nonprofit groups, and other health facilities, such as nursing homes. They also may work as independent contractors.

HISTORY

The world of health care has grown increasingly complex. New scientific discoveries allow doctors to better understand diseases and technology advancements that lead to new and better ways to treat patients. At the same time, government regulations, insurance company policies, hospital rules, and the legal field have all combined to make getting the appropriate health care a complicated process. It can sometimes seem as if the interests of patients get lost in the shuffle. It can be difficult for even the most informed patients to make sure they are getting the most beneficial treatment. This situation has led to the need for someone to work on behalf of patients, promoting their interests everywhere from the doctor's office to the Senate floor.

Although advocates for patients have existed for many years (some cite Florence Nightingale as the first advocate), the recognized profession of health advocate did not really begin do develop until the late 20th century. One step in this development was the acknowledgement by professionals that patients had rights and deserved quality treatment. An example of this occurred in 1973 when the American Hospital Association, a national organization representing hospitals, health care networks, and patients, adopted its first version of a Patient's Bill of Rights. Among other things, the bill recognizes that patients have the right to respectful care, the right to receive understandable information about their treatment, and the right to make their own decisions. Although the profession of health advocates was fairly small in the 1970s, its popularity has increased steadily since then, and health advocates have become important members of the health care community.

THE JOB

As insurance companies, doctors, and even the U.S. government do battle over the health care system, it can sometimes seem as if the interests of patients are being overlooked.

Because the world of health care has become so complex in recent years, it's difficult for even the most informed patients to make sure changes in the system will benefit them. Health advocates enter this struggle on the patients' behalf, using their own health care expertise to promote the interests of patients in the private and public sectors.

For Janet Sell, a registered oncology nurse who works at a nonprofit cancer foundation, health advocacy means working directly with individual patients to help them obtain the treatments they need. Most of Sell's clients come to her when they have been denied insurance coverage for a specific treatment, and she must find a way to reverse the decision. While most rulings arise from simple errors, sometimes insurance companies have decided that crucial treatments are unnecessary or nonstandard, and she must be extremely persistent. As Sell puts it, "You're dealing with bureaucracies. When a clerk tells you a ruling can't be altered, you can't give up until you get the results the patient needs."

For health advocates, though, getting results requires not just persistence but also strong problem-solving skills. Advocates must combine their medical and health administration expertise in creative ways, devising new negotiation strategies all the time. Often, obtaining the best possible outcome for patients means developing a specific plan for each new situation.

As Sell points out, "You have to think ahead, and you have to be strategic. If you say the wrong thing at the wrong time, you can seriously damage your chances of success, and ultimately the patient will be the one to suffer."

For Sell, the best part of advocacy is the knowledge that she is "acting on behalf of patients who desperately need assistance." Because Sell deals primarily with cancer patients, her clients often come to her once they have been significantly weakened by disease. Even patients who have educated themselves about their condition sometimes find themselves too emotionally involved to think clearly about financial or legal details. When Sell acts on behalf of these clients, she supplies both the physical stamina and the emotional distance that her patients lack. As she puts it, "I have the opportunity to do what they would do for themselves if they could."

Although Sell's position at a nonprofit organization may grant her more direct contact with her clients than advocates working to improve legislation or medical standards, to some extent all health advocates share the satisfaction of working for patients' physical and financial well-being. Unfortunately, most health advocates also share the experience that Sell identifies as the worst part of advocacy: working with government agencies involved in health care, such as Medicaid and Medicare. Even for those used to dealing with large corporations and health insurance companies, navigating the bureaucracy of governmental agencies can be a baffling task.

REQUIREMENTS

High School

If you are interested in working as a health advocate, take a broad range of classes in high school. Advocates need an extensive base of knowledge that covers medical, financial, emotional, and legal areas. Courses that are especially useful include business, mathematics, biology, health, and chemistry. Be sure to take four years of English as well as speech classes, because health advocates need strong oral and written communication skills. Learning a foreign language, such as Spanish, will also be useful. You may also want to take government, psychology, and computer science classes to prepare for this career.

Postsecondary Training

There is no single educational route to take to become a health advocate; the backgrounds that health advocates bring to the field tend to be as varied as their places of employment. Nevertheless, a knowledge of health care systems and medical terminology are important for you to have. Most employers prefer that you have at least a bachelor's degree. Some students choose to get degrees in health administration, premed, biology, or nursing. Helpful courses to take include communications, management, conflict resolution, and medical terminology. Some schools also offer classes in patient representation. As this profession has become more popular, schools are beginning to offer specialized programs of study. Sarah Lawrence College, for example, offers a master's degree in health advocacy. Course work for this degree includes nature of illness, position of the health advocate, health law, and ethics, as well as fieldwork.

Other Requirements

Advocates seem to agree that the most important training advocates can bring to this field is a sincere desire to work for the health and well-being of others. You can develop this commitment through community service, volunteer positions at hospitals, or caring for a loved one who has a serious illness. According to Marcia Hurst, head of the health advocacy program at Sarah Lawrence College, the most important skills to add to this sense of commitment are "writing, presentation skills, and analytical thinking." Though knowledge of the health care system is important, you can't do your job as an advocate unless you have the skills to convey that information in a convincing way to your audience, whether that audience is a medical ethics board or an insurance company clerk.

EXPLORING

One way to explore this field is by talking to people in it. Ask your school guidance counselor to help you set up an informational interview with a health advocate in your area. You may also be able to arrange to spend part of a day shadowing the advocate. Another way to learn more about this field is to learn about the issues that relate to patient advocacy. Visit your local library or surf the Internet to learn more. A good way to find out whether this field is for you is by volunteering at an organization that helps people. You might consider joining a religious group that helps the elderly or volunteering at a local hospital. Hospitals and nursing homes may also have paid part-time or summer positions available. Taking such a job will give you experience working in a health care environment and the opportunity to learn about patients' day-to-day needs. Stay up to date in this field by visiting related websites, such as Health Web (http://www.healthweb.org) and Healthfinder (http://www.healthfinder.gov).

EMPLOYERS

In addition to nonprofit organizations, private firms that specialize in patient advocacy have begun to spring up around the country. Some hospitals, specialty practices, and managed-care organizations now hire patient representatives to deal with patients' complaints, and corporations supporting large health care plans for their employees have begun to do the same. Advocates working on more widespread issues in the health care industry often find employment at governmental agencies, community organizations, and schools developing health advocacy courses or programs.

Job descriptions for advocates may also vary significantly, depending on your place of employment. Patient representatives employed by hospitals, doctors' groups, or large corporations still work for improved health care for patients, but also they must balance their employers' interests with those of patients. For that reason, advocates at work on the insurance or treatment side of the industry may find that their jobs resemble more typical customer service positions designed to receive and resolve consumer complaints. Advocates employed by nonprofits don't have the same responsibility to consider the financial needs of the doctors and insurance companies, and they may consequently have more freedom.

STARTING OUT

For Janet Sell, the shift from oncology nurse to patient advocate came naturally. "I wasn't a typical nurse," she remarks. "I was always more of an advocate, always complaining that things weren't right, that we could do better for the patients." Gradually, her interest in patients' rights led her to fight for legislation regarding certain treatments, and soon she made advocacy her full-time job. Sell found that her background in medicine allows her to speak with authority when confronting insurance companies and doctors.

Contact your college placement office for help in finding your first job. Some hospitals advertise job openings for health advocates in the classified section of the newspaper. You may have to start out in another position in a hospital and move into health advocacy once you've gained some experience.

ADVANCEMENT

Health advocates who work as members of a staff in a hospital can advance to department manager or other administrative positions.

Some health advocates may find jobs in hospices, in AIDS programs, or with the U.S. Department of Health and Human Services.

EARNINGS

Although independent patient advocates may have more opportunities to put the patient first, they sometimes gain that freedom at the expense of job stability and a predictable salary. Patient representatives employed by hospitals, doctors' groups, and corporations can expect to earn a regular salary of $40,000 to $60,000 a year. A self-employed patient advocate or an advocate at a private firm will likely work for consultant fees that tend to vary from job to job. Some independent patient advocates charge flat fees from $75 to $150 to analyze insurance statements; if the advocate identifies any savings for the client, the advocate and client split the savings 50-50. While these rates may work out to significant earnings per year, independent advocates have no guaranteed business, and a slow year will mean a lower income. At nonprofit organizations, advocates can rely on predictable salaries; however, because nonprofits often lack the financial wherewithal of hospitals and corporations, advocates working at nonprofits tend to earn salaries at the lower end of the pay scale.

WORK ENVIRONMENT

The type of employment that an advocate pursues largely determines their work environment. High-profile advocates striving to improve patient conditions on a national level may travel frequently, deliver speeches and seminars, and even lunch with members of Congress. Patient representatives at hospitals or managed care organizations experience a different work environment: a more standard business atmosphere, with little travel outside of the office. While it's not typical, some advocates at nonprofit or small community groups work from home. Any health advocate, though, can expect busy and varied workdays; interaction with many people is part of this job.

OUTLOOK

According to the U.S. Bureau of Labor Statistics, employment in the health services industry will increase as the population ages and new medical technologies evolve. In fact, the U.S. Department of Labor expects the number of jobs will increase by 28 percent between 2002 and 2012. While this figure includes all areas of health services, growth in health services is likely to contribute to health advocacy employment in the long run: as the number of patients increases and the field of health services becomes larger and more complex, patients' need for advocates can be expected to increase as well.

As the field of health advocacy grows, it most likely will become more established. New graduate programs can be expected to develop, and eventually undergraduate programs may exist as well. While the wide range of jobs available means that the field should stay diverse and deregulated, certain areas of health advocacy may develop certification procedures for their subgroups over the next five years.

FOR MORE INFORMATION

For information on education programs and to read selected articles from the Journal of the Health Advocacy Program, *contact*
Health Advocacy Program
Sarah Lawrence College
1 Mead Way
Bronxville, New York 10708-5999
Tel: 914-337-0700
Email: occ@mail.slc.edu
http://www.slc.edu/health_advocacy/

For general information on health advocacy careers, contact
Society for Healthcare Consumer Advocacy
American Hospital Association
One North Franklin
Chicago, IL 60606
http://www.shca-aha.org

Home Health Care Aides

OVERVIEW

Home health care aides, also known as *homemaker-home health aides* or *home attendants*, serve elderly and infirm persons by visiting them in their homes and caring for them. Working under the supervision of nurses or social workers, they perform various household chores that clients are unable to perform for themselves as well as attend to patients' personal needs. Although they work primarily with the elderly, home health care aides also attend to clients with disabilities or those needing help with small children. There are approximately 580,000 home health care aides employed in the United States.

HISTORY

Family photographs from the last century frequently included a grandparent posed alongside the children or an elderly aunt or uncle arm-in-arm with a niece or nephew. A typical household of the time often counted an elderly parent or ill or injured relative among its members. Without most of the modern conveniences we take for granted today, day-to-day living and regular household chores could be impossible for someone weakened by illness or age. It was often expected for parents to move in with children when they became unable to look after themselves; sometimes a room was prepared and waiting for them long in advance. In rural situations, elderly parents might have been expected to give up the homestead to a child or grandchild once they became incapable of looking after the place themselves.

Those without families were sometimes confined to hospitals or sanatariums. People with contagious diseases or disabilities who required constant supervision were also cared for in institutions. Even with family, however, the needs of the elderly or infirm person often exceeded the facilities, time, and energy that the family had to offer. The business of running a household left little time for the family to tend to the needs of the terminally or seriously ill.

Rural areas often made "visiting nurses" available to check on patients who lived far from town and lacked regular transportation for medical visits. These nurses eventually discovered that the needs of the patients went beyond medical care. Patients were grateful for the company of another person in their homes, someone to read their mail to them or run errands. They were grateful not to have to abandon their own homes just because they needed a little assistance from time to time. As the demand for this kind of home care advanced, home attendants found that people needed their services, and the profession of home care aides began to grow.

Advances in modern medicine have made it possible for many illnesses to be treated at home. Hospitals and stores now rent items such as wheelchairs and oxygen tanks, enabling people to have medical equipment available in their own homes. The medical profession is also learning how a person's recovery and treatment can be affected by his or her environment. People generally recover from illnesses better when they are treated in their home environment.

THE JOB

Home health care aides enable elderly persons to stay in their own homes. For some clients, just a few visits a week are enough to help them look after themselves. Although physically demanding, the work is often emotionally rewarding. Home health care aides may not have access to equipment and facilities such as those found in hospitals, but they also don't have the hospital's frantic pace. Home health care aides are expected to take the time to get to know their clients and their individual needs. They perform their duties within the client's home environment, which often is a much better atmosphere than the impersonal rooms of a hospital.

In addition to the elderly, home health care aides assist people of any age who are recovering at home following hospitalization. They also help children whose parents are ill, disabled, or neglectful. Aides may be trained to supply care to people suffering from specific illnesses such as AIDS, Alzheimer's disease, or cancer, or patients who are developmentally disabled and lack sufficient daily living skills.

Clients unable to feed themselves may depend on home health care aides to shop for food, prepare their meals, feed them, and clean up after meals. Likewise, home health care aides may assist clients in dressing and grooming, including washing, bathing, cleaning teeth and nails, and fixing the clients' hair.

Massages, alcohol rubs, whirlpool baths, and other therapies and treatments may be a part of a client's required care. Home health care aides may work closely with a physician or home nurse in giving medications and dietary supplements and helping with exercises and other therapies. They may check pulses, temperatures, and respiration rates. Occasionally, they may change nonsterile dressings, use special equipment such as a hydraulic lift, or assist with braces or artificial limbs.

Home health care aides working in home care agencies are supervised by a registered nurse, physical therapist, or social worker who assigns them specific duties. Aides report changes in patients' conditions to the supervisor or case manager.

Household chores are often another aspect of the home health care aide's responsibilities. Light housekeeping, such as changing and washing bed linens, doing the laundry and ironing, and dusting, may be necessary. When a home health care aide looks after the children of a disabled or neglectful parent, work may include making lunches for the children, helping them with their homework, or providing companionship and adult supervision in the evening.

Personal attention and comfort are important aspects of an aide's care. Home health care aides can provide this support by reading to children, playing checkers, or visiting with an elderly client. Often just listening to a client's personal problems will help the client through the day. Because elderly people do not always have the means to venture out alone, a home health care aide may accompany an ambulatory patient to the park for an afternoon stroll or to the physician's office for an appointment.

REQUIREMENTS

High School

Many programs require only a high school diploma for entry-level positions. Previous or additional course work in home economics, cooking, sewing, and meal planning are very helpful, as are courses that focus on family living and home nursing.

Postsecondary Training

Health care agencies usually focus their training on first aid, hygiene, and the principles of health care. Cooking and nutrition, including meal preparation for patients with specific dietary needs, are often included in the program. Home health care aides may take courses in psychology and child development as well as family living. Because of the need for hands-on work, aides usually learn how to bathe, dress, and feed patients as well as how to help them walk upstairs or get up from bed. The more specific the skill required for certain patients, the more an agency is likely to have more comprehensive instruction.

Most agencies will offer free training to prospective employees. Such training may include instruction on how to deal with depressed or reluctant patients, how to prepare easy and nutritious meals, and tips on housekeeping. Specific course work on health and sanitation may also be required.

Home health care aides must be willing to follow instructions and abide by the health plan created for each patient. Aides provide an important outreach service, supporting the care administered by the patient's physician, therapist, or social worker. They are not trained medical personnel, however, and must know the limits of their authority.

The federal government has enacted guidelines for home health aides whose employers receive reimbursement from Medicare. Federal law requires home health aides to pass a competency test covering 12 areas: communication skills; observation, reporting, and documentation of patient status and the care or services furnished; reading and recording vital signs; basic infection control procedures; basic elements of body function and changes; maintenance of a clean, safe, and healthy environment; recognition of and procedures for emergencies; physical, emotional, and developmental characteristics of the patients served; personal hygiene and grooming; safe transfer techniques; normal range of motion and positioning; and basic nutrition.

Federal law suggests at least 75 hours of classroom and practical training supervised by a registered nurse. Training and testing programs may be offered by the employing agency, but they must meet the standards of the Health Care Financing Administration. Training programs vary depending upon state regulations.

Certification or Licensing

The National Association for Home Care offers certification for home care and hospice executives. The certification is a voluntary demonstration that the individual has attained a defined level of education, knowledge, and experience.

Other Requirements

Caring for people in their own homes can be physically demanding work. Lifting a client for baths and exercise, helping a client up and down stairs, performing housework, and aiding with physical therapy all require that an aide be in good physical condition. Aides do not have the equipment and facilities of a hospital to help them with their work, and this requires adaptability and ingenuity. They often must make do with the resources available in a typical home.

An even temperament and a willingness to serve others are important characteristics for home health care aides. People in this occupation should be friendly, patient, sensitive to others' needs, and tactful. At times an aide will have to be stern in dealing with uncooperative patients or calm and understanding with those who are angry, confused, despondent, or in pain. Genuine warmth and respect for others are important attributes. Cheerfulness and a sense of humor can go a long way in establishing a good relationship with a client, and a good relationship can make working with the client much easier.

EXPLORING

Home health care aides are employed in many different areas. Interested students can learn more about the work by contacting local agencies and programs that provide home care services and requesting information on the organization's employment guidelines or training programs. Visiting the county or city health department and contacting the personnel director may provide useful information as well. Often, local organizations sponsor open houses to inform the community about the services they provide. This could serve as an excellent opportunity to meet the staff involved in hiring and program development and to learn about job opportunities. In addition, it may be possible to arrange to accompany a home health care aide on a home visit.

EMPLOYERS

The primary employers of home health care aides are local social service agencies that provide home care services. Such agencies often have training programs for prospective employees. Home health care aides might also find employment with hospitals that operate their own community outreach programs. Most hospitals, however, hire home health care aides through agencies.

STARTING OUT

Some social service agencies enlist the aid of volunteers. By contacting agencies and inquiring about such openings, aspiring home health care aides can get an introduction to the type of work this profession requires. Also, many agencies or nursing care facilities offer free training to prospective employees.

Checking the local Yellow Pages for agencies that provide health care to the aged and disabled or family service organizations can provide a list of employment prospects. Nursing homes, public and private health care facilities, and local chapters of the Red Cross and United Way are likely to hire entry-level employees.

ADVANCEMENT

As home health care aides develop their skills and deepen their experience, they may advance to management or supervisory positions. Those who find greater enjoyment working with clients may branch into more specialized care and pursue additional training. Additional experience and education often bring higher pay and increased responsibility.

Aides who wish to work in a clinic or hospital setting may return to school to complete a nursing degree. Other related occupations include social worker, physical or occupational therapist, and dietitian. Along with a desire for advancement, however, must come the willingness to meet additional education and experience requirements.

EARNINGS

Earnings for home health care aides are comparable to the salaries of nursing and psychiatric aides and nurse assistants. Depending on the agency, considerable flexibility exists in working hours and patient load. For many aides who begin as part-time employees, the starting salary is usually the minimum hourly wage. For full-time aides with significant training or experience, earnings may be around $7–$8 per hour. According to the U.S. Department of Labor, median hourly earnings of home health aides were $8.70 in 2002. Wages ranged from less than $6.56 to more than $12.34 an hour. Wages also vary by industry. Home health care aides who worked in community care facilities for the elderly had median earnings of $8.36, while those in individual and family services earned $8.20 an hour.

Aides are usually paid only for the time worked in the home. They normally are not paid for travel time between jobs.

WORK ENVIRONMENT

Health aides in a hospital or nursing home setting work at a much different pace and in a much different environment than the home health care aide. With home care, aides can take the time to sit with their clients and get to know them. Aides spend a certain amount of time with each client and can perform their responsibilities without the frequent distractions and demands of a hospital. Home surroundings differ from situation to situation. Some homes are neat and pleasant, while others are untidy and depressing. Some patients are angry, abusive, depressed, or otherwise difficult; others are pleasant and cooperative.

Because home health care aides usually have more than one patient, the hours an aide works can fluctuate based on the number of clients and types of services needed. Many clients may be ill or disabled. Some may be elderly and have no one else to assist them with light housekeeping or daily errands. These differences can dictate the type of responsibilities a home health care aide has for each patient.

Vacation policies and benefits packages vary with the type and size of the employing agency. Many full-time home health care aides receive one week of paid vacation following their first year of employment, and they often receive two weeks of paid vacation each year thereafter. Full-time aides may also be eligible for health insurance and retirement benefits. Some agencies also offer holiday or overtime compensation.

Working with the infirm or disabled can be a rewarding experience as aides enhance the quality of their clients' lives with their help and company. However, the personal strains—on the clients as well as the aides—can make the work challenging and occasionally frustrating. There can be difficult emotional demands that aides may find exhausting. Considerable physical activity is involved in this line of work, such as helping patients to walk, dress, or take care of themselves. Traveling from one home to another and running various errands for patients can also be tiring and time-consuming, or it can be a pleasant break in routine.

OUTLOOK

As government and private agencies develop more programs to assist the dependent, the need for home health care aides will continue to grow. Because of the physical and emotional demands of the job, there is high turnover and, therefore, frequent job openings for home health care aides.

Also, the number of people 70 years of age and older is expected to increase substantially, and many of them will require at least some home care. Rising health care costs are causing many insurance companies to consider alternatives to hospital treatment, so many insurance providers now cover home care services. In addition, hospitals and nursing homes are trying to balance the demand for their services and their limitations in staff and physical facilities. The availability of home health care aides can allow such institutions as hospitals and nursing homes to offer quality care to more people. The U.S. Department of Labor projects that employment of home health aides will grow faster than the average through 2012.

FOR MORE INFORMATION

For information on caring for the elderly, contact
ElderWeb
1305 Chadwick Drive
Normal, IL 61761
Tel: 309-451-3319
Email: info@elderweb.com
http://www.elderweb.com

For details on certification and statistics on home health care careers, contact or check out the following website:
National Association for Home Care
228 Seventh Street, SE
Washington, DC 20003
Tel: 202-547-7424
Email: membership@nahc.org
http://www.nahc.org

Home Health Care and Hospice Nurses

OVERVIEW

Home health care nurses, also called *visiting nurses*, provide home-based health care under the direction of a physician. They care for persons who may be recovering from an accident, illness, surgery, cancer, or childbirth. They may work for a community organization, a private health care provider, or they may be independent nurses who work on a contract basis.

While home health care nurses care for patients expecting to recover, *hospice nurses* care for people who are in the final stages of a terminal illness. Typically, a hospice patient has less than six months to live. Hospice nurses provide medical and emotional support to the patients and their families and friends. Hospice care usually takes place in the patient's home, but patients may also receive hospice care in a hospital room, nursing home, or a relative's home. The National Hospice and Palliative Care Organization states, "Hospice care professionals and volunteers provide services that address all of the symptoms of a terminal illness—ranging from physical to emotional to spiritual—with the aim of promoting comfort and dignity and living as fully as possible at life's end."

Both home health care and hospice nursing professions practice a team approach in caring for their patients. Support people, such as volunteers, aides, therapists, social workers, and clergy, are often involved in the patient's care, as well as doctors. There are approximately 615,000 home health care workers employed in the United States.

HISTORY

Home health care originated with the Visiting Nurse Agencies more than 110 years ago. At that time, the need was critical; there were few hospitals to serve many communities, and where they existed, they usually cared only for those who were seriously ill.

Generally, patients were cared for by their families at home. The introduction of trained medical professionals into the household not only improved the quality of medical care available, but brought compassion and support to help both the patient and the family.

Though they were originally intended to serve communities without adequate health care, home health care and hospice nurses are now in demand for another reason. Today, as patients spend less time in the hospital and as more medical procedures are done on an outpatient basis, the need for professional follow-up care in the home is essential. Recovery, rehabilitation, and care for illnesses and injuries are happening in the home. According to the Visiting Nurse Associations of America, visiting nurses care for nearly 4 million people every year.

THE JOB

Home health care nurses are often assigned to patients after the patients are discharged from a hospital or after they have had outpatient procedures. They provide follow-up health care on a regular basis and establish a one-on-one patient/nurse relationship. Some home health care nurses also work with patients who have acute, ongoing illnesses such as diabetes or high blood pressure.

According to Joan Bissing, RN, BS, a hospice nurse in California, "[Home health care nurses and hospice nurses] often provide wound care, draw blood, and give medications. We may also do chemotherapy, or IV therapy."

"It is essential that a hospice or home health care nurse have nursing experience before going into this specialty," Bissing states. "While most nurses work directly under a doctor, hospice and home health care nurses must have a specialty in high-tech nursing and a knowledge of different diseases since they are often required to work independently."

Although they need to be able to work alone, nurses in this specialty must also know how to work as a member of a team. A variety of hospice personnel, such as doctors, social workers, chaplains, volunteers, counselors, and aides, become involved with the patient as the illness progresses. Home health care and hospice nurses work with all aspects and ages of the population. Their duties vary greatly depending on their patients, their illnesses, and the care or support they need.

Sometimes the job requires the nurse to "just listen," says Bissing. "We can sometimes sense that our terminally ill patient is unsettled about something, such as past relationships, and then we need to be proactive and get the proper counseling or clergy to help the patient deal with the problem and find peace."

The hospice nurse is often a source of comfort to the patient and his or her family and friends. "Some patients may say, I've had enough treatments. I just want to live my final days as peacefully and pain free as possible," Bissing says. The hospice nurse must work with the hospice team to make sure those wishes are carried out. "At that point, we focus on giving the patient the best quality of life we can, keeping the patient as comfortable and pain free as possible."

There are rewards to every member of the hospice team, according to Bissing. "They all learn something from each of their patients. Sometimes it is an experience they won't ever forget." She goes on, "It can be as simple as a touch of the hand with a difficult patient, or as complex as facilitating a reunion with a long-lost relative before the patient's death."

One thing Bissing wants anyone thinking of going into this profession to remember, "Never forget that it's okay to cry. Shared tears are often part of the patient care."

REQUIREMENTS

High School
To prepare for a career in nursing, take as many science and math courses as possible, especially classes in biology and chemistry. English and writing classes will foster the communication skills that are vital to this career.

Postsecondary Training
Nurses who specialize in a specific nursing field such as home health care or hospice nursing must first become registered nurses. The three main paths to a career as a registered nurse are obtaining a bachelor of science degree in nursing from a four-year college or university, obtaining an associate's degree in nursing from a two-year college or technical school, or obtaining a diploma from a nursing school. Obtaining a bachelor's degree in nursing is considered the best preparation for this career, as it provides a broad range of experience in different types of nursing.

Many home health care and hospice nurses are required to have some nursing experience, preferably in acute care, because they are required to work with patients with a wide range of health problems. Entry-level requirements depend on the home health care agency, the hospice organization, and the availability of nurses in that specialty and geographical region.

Certification or Licensing
All registered nurses must be licensed to work in the state in which they are employed. They must graduate from an accredited nursing program and pass a national licensing examination to obtain this license. Nurses who wish to specialize in hospice or home health care may choose to attend graduate school.

As with almost all health care professions today, nurses spend a great deal of time keeping records and charts and documenting the services they provide in order to meet insurance, government, and Medicare requirements.

Other Requirements
Home health care and hospice nurses should feel comfortable working with patients of all ages and people from all cultural backgrounds. Good communication skills are essential, including the ability to listen and respond to the patients' needs. Home health care and hospice nurses must be able to work independently, have good organizational skills, and also have the ability to supervise aides and other support people. Flexibility is also a requirement because duties vary greatly from hour to hour and day to day. Many hospice nurses are on call and their work is mentally stressful. "There is a lot of burnout in hospice nursing," confirms Joan Bissing. "Hospice nurses usually don't stay in the field long. It is hard work and very intense. Much of hospice nursing is treating the symptoms of the disease, rather than curing the disease."

EXPLORING

There are many ways to explore the field of nursing while in high school. Check out your school or local library to read books on nursing careers. You can also arrange to talk with your high school guidance counselor, school nurse, and even local public health nurses. Consider visiting a hospital to observe nurses at work and to talk with personnel. You may be able to work as a volunteer. Other volunteer work experiences may be found with the Red Cross or community health services.

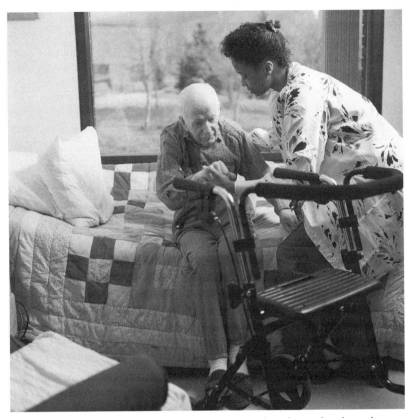

Home health care nurses must be able to work independently and work flexible hours. *(Getty Images)*

To explore the career of home health care and hospice nursing, try contacting local agencies and programs that provide home care services and request information on employment guidelines or training programs. Home health organizations may sponsor open houses to enlighten the community to the services they provide. This could allow you to meet the staff involved in hiring and program development and to learn about job opportunities. Finally, ask if it may be possible to accompany a home health care or hospice nurse on a home visit.

EMPLOYERS

According to the National Association for Home Care, there are more than 20,000 home health care providers in the United States. As of 2002, there were approximately 3,200 hospices in operation in the United States. These health care providers often have training pro-grams for prospective employees. Home health care and hospice nurses might also find employment with hospitals that operate their own community outreach programs. Most hospitals, however, hire through agencies.

STARTING OUT

Once registered, nurses may apply for employment directly to hos-pitals, nursing homes, companies, and government agencies that hire nurses. Home care and hospice jobs can also be obtained through school placement offices, employment agencies specializing in place-ment of nursing personnel, or state employment offices. Other sources of jobs include nurses' associations, professional journals, and news-paper want ads.

For a list of employment prospects, check the local Yellow Pages for agencies that provide health care to the aged and disabled or fam-ily service. Many agencies or nursing care facilities offer free train-ing to qualified employees.

ADVANCEMENT

Additional experience and education often bring higher pay and increased responsibility. Home health care and hospice nurses may advance to management or supervisory positions. Those who would rather continue to work with clients may branch into more special-ized care or a related field and pursue additional training. Other pos-sible fields include social work, physical or occupational therapy, and dietetics.

EARNINGS

According to the U.S. Department of Labor's *Occupational Outlook Handbook*, median annual earnings of registered nurses were $48,090 in 2002. Salaries ranged from less than $33,970 to more than $69,670. The Department of Labor also notes that nurses working in home health care services have a median salary of $45,890 per year.

Salary is determined by many factors, including nursing specialty, education, place of employment, geographical location, and work experience. Flexible schedules are available for most full-time nurs-es, and part-time work is often available. Employers usually provide health and life insurance, and some offer educational reimburse-ments and year-end bonuses to their full-time staff.

WORK ENVIRONMENT

Most hospice and home health care nurses care for their patients in the patients' homes, nursing homes, or in the homes of their caregivers, so the work environment can be as varied as their patients' lifestyles. In addition, patients and family members can be very tense during this stressful period of their lives and they may be unpleasant and uncooperative at times. Some nurses are on call 24 hours a day and may be required to travel to homes in all neighborhoods of a city or in remote rural areas day and night. Safety may be an issue at times.

All nursing careers have some health and disease risks; however, adherence to health and safety guidelines greatly minimizes the chance of contracting infectious diseases such as hepatitis and AIDS. Medical knowledge and good safety measures are also needed to limit the nurse's exposure to toxic chemicals, radiation, and other hazards.

OUTLOOK

According to the U.S. Department of Labor, there will be more new jobs for registered nurses than for any other occupation through 2012. In addition, the unemployment rate for all nursing professions reported by the American Association of Critical Care Nurses is less than 2 percent. Part-time job opportunities are also plentiful in the nursing profession.

The nursing demand will be felt particularly in the hospice and home health care fields. The U.S. Bureau of the Census estimates that the number of individuals aged 65 or older will double by 2030. As the older population increases, their need for medical care will also increase. Hospice participation has grown at a dramatic rate, especially among those involved with Medicare. This number is expected to increase as the population ages and health care costs rise.

FOR MORE INFORMATION

For information on becoming a home health care or hospice nurse, contact the following organizations:

American Association of Colleges of Nursing
One Dupont Circle, NW, Suite 530
Washington, DC 20036
Tel: 202-463-6930
http://www.aacn.nche.edu

National Association for Home Care
228 Seventh Street, SE
Washington, DC 20003
Tel: 202-547-7424
http://www.nahc.org

National Hospice and Palliative Care Organization
1700 Diagonal Road, Suite 625
Alexandria, VA 22314
Tel: 703-837-1500
Email: nhpco_info@nhpco.org
http://www.nhpco.org

Visiting Nurse Associations of America
99 Summer Street, Suite 1700
Boston, MA 02110
Tel: 617-737-3200
Email: vnaa@vnaa.org
http://www.vnaa.org

Hospice Workers

OVERVIEW

Hospice workers provide support for terminally ill patients in the final stages of their illness. Hospice care is a benefit under Medicare Hospital Insurance and eligible persons can receive medical and support services for their terminal illnesses. Care is primarily provided in the patients' homes, but may also be provided in nursing homes and hospitals, with the intent to make patients as comfortable and pain-free as medically possible during the final days of their lives. A team of specially trained professionals and volunteers provides hospice care. The National Hospice and Palliative Care Organization (NHPCA) estimates that approximately 885,000 patients are served by hospice organizations each year.

HISTORY

The hospice concept can be traced to ancient times when shelter and rest (hospitality) were provided for travelers. Home care has also been a tradition in America since the 1880s when public health nurses began traveling to patients' homes to care for the sick and comfort the dying. However, the term *hospice* was first used in 1967 to mean specialized care for dying patients when St. Christopher's Hospice in a residential suburb of London was established. The first hospice in the United States, The Connecticut Hospice, was established in 1974. Today, hospice refers to a type of compassionate care and support given to the dying patient and to the patient's family and caregivers. There are approximately 3,200 organizations that provide hospice services in the United States.

QUICK FACTS

School Subjects
Health
Psychology

Personal Skills
Helping/teaching
Technical/scientific

Work Environment
Primarily indoors
Primarily one location

Minimum Education Level
High school diploma

Salary Range
Varies according to position

Certification or Licensing
Required for certain
  positions

Outlook
Faster than the average

DOT
N/A

GOE
N/A

NOC
N/A

O*NET-SOC
N/A

THE JOB

Hospice workers help patients who have a variety of terminal illnesses and who can no longer benefit from curative treatment. Typically, a hospice patient has less than six months to live.

Hospice workers are a team of trained professionals that include administrators, physicians, nurses, counselors, chaplains, therapists, social workers, aides, and volunteers. Hospice organizations rely heavily on volunteers, who must participate in intensive volunteer training. According to a study by the National Hospice and Palliative Care Association of America, the more than 400,000 hospice volunteers in the United States contribute almost 13 percent of the clinical hours provided to hospice patients and families.

Hospices use a team approach to plan and coordinate care for the patient. This team includes the patient, family, and the hospice team, all working together. Family or primary caregivers can call for the help of a hospice team member 24 hours a day, seven days a week, and a team member will respond whenever needed.

Hospice workers' job responsibilities are related to their profession. Hospice *medical directors* may be licensed *physicians* who oversee the medical program and advise the hospice care staff. *Registered nurses* may be responsible for seeing that a member of the hospice team meets the patient's needs. Nurses also visit patients to monitor their emotional and physical symptoms. *Nurse assistants* and *home health care aides* assist the family in the personal care of the patient such as bathing, grooming, and changing the bed linens. *Physical, occupational,* and *speech therapists* help patients with daily living tasks that have become difficult or impossible to perform. *Social workers* help the patient and family deal with the emotions surrounding the illness. They also help locate personal and community resources that may assist the patient or the family. *Volunteer coordinators* are responsible for organizing and directing the volunteer program and for training the volunteer workers. *Chaplains* provide religious support to the patient and family in accordance with their specific religious beliefs. *Music therapists* use music to provide comfort and relaxation to the patient. *Grief therapists* help the family deal with the death of their loved one and cope with their grief.

REQUIREMENTS

High School

Persons wishing to obtain a college degree in one of the professions employed by hospice organizations should take a well-balanced college preparatory course in high school, with a good foundation in the sciences. Biology, chemistry, and psychology are important courses. You should take anatomy and physiology if your high school offers these courses. You should also take courses in the humanities and social sciences, as well as classes that improve communication skills.

High school diploma requirements vary with hospice organizations and the volunteer responsibilities. Some volunteer work for example, answering the phones, cleaning, or maintaining grounds, does not require a diploma of any kind. However, a high school diploma would probably be required for any volunteer position that involves patient contact.

Postsecondary Training

The degree program you should pursue depends on the role you hope to play in the hospice programs. Some positions require a bachelor's degree and others a medical degree or other specialized degree. Although only a few colleges and universities offer specialized hospice degrees, many hospitals do offer medical rotations in hospice care to physicians, nurses, and other professionals involved in training.

Certification or Licensing

The certification or licensing requirements are determined by the medical specialty or professional career that you wish to pursue. The hospice itself is usually licensed by the department of health of each state (more than 40 states license hospice programs) and certified by Medicare and Medicaid.

Other Requirements

If you are planning to become involved in hospice care, you should be able to work as a member of a team to provide the support and care that is needed by terminally ill patients and their loved ones and caregivers. You should be compassionate, patient, sensitive, and well organized. Flexibility and the ability to make decisions are important. You should also feel comfortable dealing with the sick and dying.

EMPLOYERS

Hospice organizations hire hospice workers and also welcome hospice volunteers. As of 2002, there were approximately 3,200 hospice programs in all 50 states, the District of Columbia, and Puerto Rico. Half of these hospices operate as independent entities, while

Managing Stress in Hospice Work

Because hospice workers help dying people and their families make the most of the time they have together, their work can be incredibly rewarding and fulfilling. But at the same time, hospice workers must—on a daily basis—remain compassionate and reassuring in intensely emotional moments. This can result in a lot of stress and anxiety for the hospice worker. Helen Fitzgerald, the training director for the American Hospice Foundation, recommends the following ways for hospice workers to maintain their own emotional and physical well-being as they help their patients and patient families do the same:

Say good-bye: A unique and challenging aspect of hospice work is knowing that the patient is in the last months or weeks of his or her life. The hospice worker must be able to say good-bye to patients that may have become good friends, and they must encourage the patient and their family to do the same to each other when the time comes.

Allow grief: It is important for hospice workers to allow themselves a period of grieving when a patient passes. Only after this will the hospice worker be able to meet the needs of his or her next assignment. Creative outlets such as writing, painting, or playing music often help people through the grief process.

Tend to basic health needs: Although they are also responsible for the physical and mental needs of their patients, hospice workers must allow time for their own rest, exercise, and proper nutrition. This aids the mental and physical balance they need to perform their jobs.

Nurture relationships: Hospice workers should cultivate enriching personal and social relationships outside of work. This helps the hospice worker to maintain a sense of individuality apart from the serious duties of this profession.

Attend in-house meetings: Meeting with other hospice workers to discuss the workday and "blow off steam" is another important step for hospice workers to remain balanced and focused.

Make relaxation a priority: From classes and exercise to meditation or shopping at the mall, hospice workers must make a point of pursuing leisure activities they enjoy in order to release some of the stress and pressure they experience on the job.

Source: American Hospice Foundation, http://www.americanhospice.org/griefzone/articles/hospicestress.htm

others are associated with hospitals, home health agencies, and nursing facilities. The majority of hospices (69 percent) are non-profit organizations.

STARTING OUT

If you are interested in pursuing a career as a hospice worker, you should consider doing volunteer work at a hospice center, hospital, or nursing home when in high school. This will give you an insight into the hospice environment and its career possibilities.

If you choose to complete professional training, a placement office associated with your degree program may help you locate employment opportunities. In addition, contacts you made in clinical settings while training or volunteering may be helpful. Applying directly to hospices and other health care agencies and answering ads in professional journals can also produce employment opportunities.

ADVANCEMENT

Advancement opportunities include director and supervisor positions within the hospice program. Other career opportunities may exist with government agencies and organizations associated with hospice and home health care programs. A degree may be required to advance to some positions.

EARNINGS

Salaries for hospice workers are similar to those of their counterparts in a more typical medical setting and generally are based on the position, the educational requirements for that position, and the level of experience of the worker. According to the *2001–02 Hospice Salary and Benefits Report* conducted by the Hospital and Healthcare Compensation Service, median salaries for an executive director ranged from $51,050 to $100,450, depending on the size of the facility. The median salary for executive directors in home care was $63,882. The median salary for a director of social work and counseling was $41,900, while the median salary for a director of nursing/clinical services was $51,497 in 1999.

Hospice chaplains, music therapists, and grief therapists may earn salaries that range from $20,000 to $35,000 annually.

The *Occupational Outlook Handbook* reports the following average salaries in 2002 for health care and human services workers that are involved in hospice work: licensed practical nurses, $31,440;

registered nurses, $48,090; home health aides, $18,096; physical therapists, $57,330; medical social workers, $37,380.

Fringe benefits are usually similar to those of other full-time health care workers and may include sick leave, vacation, health and life insurance, and tuition assistance.

WORK ENVIRONMENT

Most hospice workers visit terminally ill patients in their homes or in the homes of their caregivers so the work environment can be as varied as their patients' lifestyles. Some workers are on call 24 hours a day and may be required to travel to homes in all areas of a city or rural area to provide medical and supportive care. Patients and family members can be very tense during this stressful period in their lives, and they may be unpleasant and uncooperative at times. As with any health care profession, hospice workers have the possibility of exposure to contagious diseases; however, proper precautions and training diminish this risk.

OUTLOOK

Hospice participation has grown at a dramatic rate, especially among those involved with Medicare. According to the National Association of Home Care, from 1984 to 2000 the total number of hospices participating in Medicare rose from 31 to 2,288—nearly a 75-fold increase. The number of hospices and patients serviced by them is expected to increase as the population ages and health care costs rise. In addition, according to the Hospice Association of America, families and medical professionals are choosing hospice care because of its holistic, patient-family, in-home-centered philosophy.

FOR MORE INFORMATION

For information on hospice centers and careers, contact the following organizations:

Hospice Education Institute
3 Unity Square
PO Box 98
Machiasport, MA 04655-0098
Tel: 800-331-1620
Email: info@hospiceworld.org
http://www.hospiceworld.org

National Association for Home Care
228 Seventh Street, SE
Washington, DC 20003
Tel: 202-547-7424
Email: membership@nahc.org
http://www.nahc.org

National Hospice and Palliative Care Organization
1700 Diagonal Road, Suite 625
Alexandria, VA 22314
Tel: 703-837-1500
Email: nhpco_info@nhpco.org
http://www.nhpco.org

Nursing Home Administrators

OVERVIEW

Nursing home administrators are responsible for the management of nursing homes. Their duties are wide ranging, covering everything from keeping track of financial accounts to making sure the facility is up to code to greeting residents at social events. In addition, administrators supervise managers throughout the residence. *Nursing home managers* head different departments of a facility, such as housekeeping, dietary, human resources, and they report any problems or needs to the nursing home administrator, who then addresses the situation. Administrators work closely with the medical director and nursing staff to ensure proper medical treatment for all residents. They also act as the nursing home's representative during interactions with residents' families, government agencies, and the community.

HISTORY

Institutions for the elderly have not always been clean and cheery places. Nevertheless, such institutions have existed in the United States since colonial times. One such institution was the poor house, modeled after the English almshouse. Elderly people without means of support or families to care for them often ended up living their final days in these dismal places. Religious institutions, such as convents, also offered places for the old and sick to stay. And, of course, families provided care for their senior members, often with several generations living in one household.

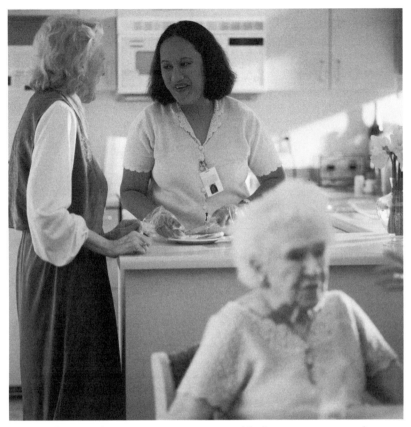

Nursing home administrators are responsible for every aspect of running their facility, from setting budgets to making sure residents are comfortable and happy. *(Getty Images)*

It was not until the 20th century, however, that the long-term care of seniors became organized into a business. According to the American Health Care Association, the first nursing homes in the United States came into existence around 1900. Originally these homes were boarding houses, places where people paid rent that covered rooms and meals. As boarding house residents aged, some became physically unable to care for themselves and needed help with everyday activities. In addition, those without other family members, who otherwise would take care of them, sought places that offered basic medical care in addition to meals and lodging. Boarding house owners recognized the need to provide housing and medical services for these older residents. Those who began to supply these services became the first people to run nursing homes and were, essentially, the first nursing home administrators.

By 1920, state health departments developed licensure programs for nursing homes within their jurisdiction to better regulate facilities and their services. The 1930s saw the development of the Social Security and Old Age Assistance programs, government programs designed to give the elderly financial support that they could use for their care. In 1965 the programs Medicare and Medicaid were added to the Social Security Act. These two programs paid providers of care services directly and helped to spur the growth of the long-term care industry.

Today, as the country's senior population expands, as medical and technological advances are made, and as lifestyles change, the need for well-managed, comfortable, clean, and affordable long-term care for the elderly is greater than ever.

THE JOB

The term *nursing home* usually makes people think of what are called skilled nursing facilities. These facilities provide 24-hour nursing care, meals, and living space to residents. Many nursing home administrators work at skilled nursing facilities. However, other types of nursing or care facilities also exist. For example, intermediate-care facilities, which provide residents with meals and shelter and may also provide regular medical care, although not on a 24-hour basis, employ administrators. And administrators work at residential care facilities, also called assisted living facilities. These facilities provide residents with meals and living space but offer only limited medical supervision and care.

In addition to these three distinctions (skilled nursing, intermediate care, and residential care facilities), nursing homes can also be grouped into three categories based on their ownership. Not-for-profit nursing homes are run by voluntary organizations, such as fraternal or religious groups. Proprietary facilities are those run for profit by individuals, partnerships, or corporations. And government facilities are run, of course, by the government and include such places as veterans' homes and state-run nursing homes.

However, no matter what type of facility they work for and no matter who owns the facility, all nursing home administrators are responsible for every aspect of maintaining and operating that home. Their many duties range from management of personnel to public relations. Depending on the size of the facility, administrators may have one or more assistants to help with the daily responsibilities.

If the nursing home is part of a large corporation, the administrator must meet with the governing board or other administrators from different facilities within the company. They take an active role in helping plan budgets and programs. For example, if staff resources are low or new equipment or remodeling is needed, the administrator must explain the situation to the corporate office in order to get proper funding for the project. They may also help set fee schedules for patient services.

Lynn Cecconi is a nursing home administrator. Her facility is one of many owned and operated by a health care group in the Chicago area. "I have a monthly meeting with corporate to explain the numbers," says Cecconi, referring to the facility's budget. If the nursing home spends more than the budget allowed, Cecconi must explain where and how the funds were allotted. If the nursing home spends less than the budget allowed, that too must be explained. "I am accountable for everything."

Administrators oversee every department in the nursing home from dietary to medical records. Some departments may have their own managers, but these managers must report to the administrator. Many times, administrators interview and hire department managers; they also have a voice in how staff members are trained and supervised. Administrators also work with the medical director and nursing director to plan medical policies and procedures that will ensure the best health care for all the residents. They also work with the

Words to Know

adult home: senior citizens' home that provides meals, personal care services, and private or semi-private rooms, but no medical services

assisted living: combines enriched housing and nursing care services

congregate care: general term for senior citizen housing with some care services

enriched housing: an adult home with individual apartments and no personal care services

independent living: housing for the well elderly, which may include housekeeping and some meal services; housing may be apartments, cottages, condos, etc.

life care retirement community: provides the full range of living options for the elderly, from independent living to nursing homes

Source: Health Advocates for Older People Inc., http://www.hafopinc.org/glossary.html

activities director in planning recreational events, holiday parties, and other year-round entertainment for the residents.

Administrators are responsible for dealing with different government agencies that monitor health care. Nursing homes must meet strict guidelines before becoming Medicare and/or Medicaid certified by the federal agency Centers for Medicare and Medicaid Services (CMS). Without CMS approval, Medicare and Medicaid will not pay for any services rendered at the facility. In addition, every nursing home facility undergoes an annual inspection by the state's health department. Any discrepancies or violations found are directed to the administrator for explanation. Many nursing homes also participate in voluntary quality assurance programs that measure the performance of the facility and its staff.

If there are problems with the staff, or complaints regarding a client's treatment or well-being, the administrator must intervene. A good administrator should be able to listen, assess the situation, and act accordingly. Administrators should not only be visible to patients and their families, but be approachable as well. For Cecconi, the most important duty of a nursing home administrator is "assuring positive resident outcome." She works closely with her staff to make sure every resident is well cared for and happy. Cecconi finds that if the resident is treated well, then the families are satisfied.

REQUIREMENTS

High School

Are you thinking about a career in health administration? If you are, you should know that there are several key classes to include in your high school curriculum. Managing a nursing home is very similar to managing a business. Classes such as accounting, business management, and computer science will help prepare you for the business side of this job. Quantitative skills are needed to excel in this career, so make sure you take as many math classes as possible. Science and health classes are important to take and will prepare you for college. High school classes in sociology, psychology, and social studies can provide you with a background for understanding a variety of people. And, because you will be working with so many different people and must give directions, take English, speech, and foreign language classes to hone your communication and leadership skills.

Postsecondary Training

Most nursing home administrators have a college degree in health administration, business, human resources, or another related field.

A few states do allow licensing for administrators who hold an associate's degree and have a certain amount of experience. It is recommended, however, that you get a bachelor's degree. One reason for this is that requirements for professional certification stipulate that anyone licensed after 1996 must also hold a bachelor's degree to be eligible for certification. In addition, most employers insist on hiring only those with at least a bachelor's degree.

Many colleges and universities across the United States offer bachelor's degrees in health care administration, health service administration, or long-term care administration with concentrations or minors in nursing home management. The Association of University Programs in Health Administration (AUPHA) certifies undergraduate programs that meet the organization's standards; the National Association of Boards of Examiners of Long Term Care Administrators grants academic approval to undergraduate programs in long-term care administration. For information on certified and approved programs, contact these organizations (see the end of this article for addresses and websites). The Accrediting Commission on Education for Health Services Administration is the accrediting body for graduate programs in health administration education. Information on these graduate programs is also available from the AUPHA. Graduates of advanced-degree programs usually have a master's of science in health administration or a master's in business administration in health care management.

Courses you are likely to take as an undergraduate cover subjects such as health law, gerontology, medical terminology, and health care financial management. In addition, expect to take classes such as accounting, marketing, computer science, and organizational theory. Some programs also require students to complete an internship, also called an administrator-in-training program.

Certification or Licensing

Professional certification is available from the American College of Health Care Administrators. Certification requirements include having a bachelor's degree, having two years of professional experience as a nursing home administrator, completing a certain amount of continuing education, and passing the certification exam. Candidates who meet all requirements receive the designation certified nursing home administrator (CNHA). Certification demonstrates an administrator's level of experience and professionalism and is recommended.

All nursing home administrators must be licensed. All states and the District of Columbia require candidates to pass a national licensing exam given by the National Association of Boards of Examiners of Long Term Care Administrators. In addition, many states require candidates to pass a state exam as well as to fulfill certain requirements, such as having completed an administrator-in-training program of a certain length and completing a certain number of continuing education hours. Since these state requirements vary, you will need to check with the licensing board of the state in which you hope to work for specific information.

Other Requirements

Nursing home administrators must have a keen sense for business and enjoy managing people, budgets, and resources. They should be able to work well with a wide variety of people, from government officials to residents' families. But just as important as having a feel for business, nursing home administrators must have a special interest in helping people, especially the elderly. Administrators need to be aware of the emotional and physical challenges their residents face and be able to figure out ways to make their facilities accommodating. Administrators need to have a positive attitude and to be committed to lifelong learning, since continuing education is an essential part of this work.

EXPLORING

To explore the field of nursing home administration, try contacting a nursing home in your area and make an appointment to speak with the administrator or assistant administrator about this work. They should be able to answer any questions you may have about the job, as well as give you a feel for their workday.

Hands-on experience is also important, so volunteer at a local nursing home or assisted living residence. You can help conduct activities such as games, arts and crafts, holiday celebrations, reading aloud to the sight impaired, or simply keeping lonely seniors company. Most, if not all, facilities welcome volunteers. In addition, there may be opportunities for paid part-time or summer jobs at these facilities. Even if you end up only working in the kitchen, you will still get a good feel for the structure of the business.

EMPLOYERS

There are about 19,000 nursing homes located throughout the United States. Each nursing home, depending on its size, needs administrators and assistant administrators to oversee its operation.

Not-for-profit groups, corporations, and government agencies employ administrators in a variety of settings: at skilled nursing, intermediate care, and residential facilities. No matter what the facility is, however, each needs administrative leadership to ensure successful operation.

Do job opportunities vary from state to state? According to the 2000 Census conducted by the U.S. Census Bureau, California had the largest number of residents age 60 and over, with approximately 4.7 million. Alaska, on the other hand, ranked at the bottom with approximately 53,000 residents in this age group. It makes sense to conclude that opportunities for nursing home employment are most plentiful in areas with high concentrations of older residents.

STARTING OUT

A nursing home administrator is considered a high executive position, so it is quite rare to land this job directly after graduation. Working as an assistant administrator is a more realistic mid-level management position. It is not uncommon for administrators to have one or more assistants responsible for different aspects of running the nursing home, especially at larger facilities. For example, one assistant administrator may be in charge of human resources and benefits, while another is assigned to keeping inventory and purchasing supplies. The administrator oversees the work of each assistant.

As a starting point for the career of administrator, however, you may begin as an activity director or, depending on the size of the facility, as an assistant to the activity director. Nursing home patients look forward to a variety of diversions to help make their stay pleasant and enjoyable. Coordinating weekly patient entertainment, such as bingo, arts and crafts, holiday parties, and other celebrations, are some of the duties of an activity director.

Other routes into this field include jobs that familiarize you with government agencies and case management. In Lynn Cecconi's situation, her past experience working as a discharge planner and as a public aid caseworker gave her valuable training in working with both Medicare and Medicaid. Her ability to navigate through these two complicated government agencies and their policies gave Cecconi an edge over other candidates.

ADVANCEMENT

It is hard to identify a typical route of advancement for the nursing home administrator, since this is already considered an executive position. Experienced administrators might choose to work for a larger nursing home with a bigger staff. If employed by a chain, administrators may advance by being transferred to other nursing home locations or promoted to the corporate office. Administrative positions at hospitals, health maintenance organizations, pharmaceutical companies, or national associations, such as the Red Cross, are other options for advancement. The skills and experience nursing home administrators possess, such as management and budgeting, can be easily applied to other areas of the corporate world.

EARNINGS

According to the 2001 *Nursing Home Salary and Benefits Survey* conducted by the Hospital and Healthcare Compilation Service, nursing home administrators earned a national average of $67,666 annually, plus an average year-end bonus of $7,803. This same survey finds assistant administrators earned a national average of $50,562 annually, plus an average bonus of $2,327. It is important to note, however, that not all nursing homes give year-end bonuses, and the smart employee never counts on a bonus. The U.S. Department of Labor reported a median annual income of $55,320 in 2002 for medical and health services managers working at nursing and personal care facilities, a category including nursing home administrators. Ten percent of all medical and health services managers earned less than $37,460, and 10 percent earned more than $109,080 in 2002. These salaries do not include bonuses. Income also depends on the administrator's experience, the size of the facility, its ownership, and its location in the country.

Administrators receive added benefits such as health and life insurance, paid vacation and sick time, and retirement plans.

WORK ENVIRONMENT

Most administrators are scheduled for eight-hour workdays, although they often work longer hours, especially when there are a large number of admissions or if there is a problem that needs to be addressed. Administrators must be available at all hours to handle any emergency that may arise. Most keep a regular Monday through Friday work schedule; some work on weekends. Lynn Cecconi is often at the nursing home on important holidays, such as Thanksgiving or Christmas, to greet the residents and their families as well as the staff.

Administrators usually have private offices, but the nature of their job takes them to every department and floor of the nursing home facility. If there is a problem in the dietary department, the administrator must go to the dietitian's office or the kitchen. A resident's complaint may take the administrator to that particular room.

Most nursing home facilities do not enforce a dress code for non-medical staff. However, it is important to dress professionally and in a manner appropriate to the environment.

OUTLOOK

Nursing home administration, like many careers in geriatric care, is a field to watch. According to the U.S. Department of Labor, employment of health service managers is expected to grow faster than the average through 2012. Much of the anticipated employment opportunities will be at nursing homes and other residential facilities.

One reason for this demand will be the increased number of seniors. The U.S. Census Bureau projects there will be approximately 70 million older persons, age 65 years or older, by 2030. This age group will grow dramatically beginning in 2010, when the baby boom generation (those born from the mid-1940s to the mid-1960s) reaches senior status.

People are also living longer than ever before due to improvements in medical care and healthier lifestyles. As life expectancies rise, many families are presented with the unique situation of caring for their elderly parents, and sometimes their grandparents, while raising their own young families.

Another reason nursing home facilities and those who work in them will be in demand is our mobile society. People relocate today much more than in generations past, often moving away from their original homes for better employment opportunities. It is not uncommon for the elderly to have no immediate family members living close by. The primary reason many senior citizens enter nursing homes is their inability to care for themselves due to chronic illness or advanced age. According to a study conducted by Columbia University College of Physicians and Surgeons, the "typical" nursing home resident's stay is two and a half years. As the number of people requiring round-the-clock medical attention increases, so will the need for more nursing home facilities. This, in turn, will fuel a demand for qualified nursing home administrators.

FOR MORE INFORMATION

For information regarding not-for-profit facilities, contact
American Association of Homes and Services for the Aging
2519 Connecticut Avenue, NW
Washington, DC 20008-1520
Tel: 202-783-2242
http://www.aahsa.org

For information on careers, certification, and licensure, contact the following organizations:
American College of Health Care Administrators
300 North Lee Street, Suite 301
Alexandria, VA 22314
Tel: 888-882-2422
Email: education@achca.org
http://www.achca.org

American College of Healthcare Executives
One North Franklin Street, Suite 1700
Chicago, IL 60606-4425
Tel: 312-424-2800
http://www.ache.org

For information regarding long-term health care and its facilities in the United States, contact
American Health Care Association
1201 L Street, NW
Washington, DC 20005
Tel: 202-842-4444
http://www.ahca.org

Contact the AUPHA for information regarding accredited academic programs in health administration.
Association of University Programs in Health Administration (AUPHA)
2000 North 14th Street, Suite 780
Arlington, VA 22201
Tel: 202-638-1448
Email: aupha@aupha.org
http://www.aupha.org

For information on licensing and undergraduate degree programs in long-term care administration, visit the following website:

National Association of Boards of Examiners of Long Term Care Administrators
1444 I Street, NW, Suite 700
Washington, DC 20005
Tel: 202-712-9040
http://www.nabweb.org

For career information, visit the following website:
Long Term Care Education
http://www.longtermcareeducation.com

Orientation and Mobility Specialists

QUICK FACTS

School Subjects
Health
Psychology

Personal Skills
Communication/ideas
Helping/teaching

Work Environment
Primarily indoors
Primarily multiple locations

Minimum Education Level
Bachelor's degree

Salary Range
$23,840 to $37,380 to
$56,320

Certification or Licensing
Required by certain states

Outlook
Faster than the average

DOT
076

GOE
10.02.02

NOC
4215

O*NET-SOC
N/A

OVERVIEW

Orientation and mobility specialists help people with disabilities stay actively involved in society. They teach blind, visually impaired, and disabled individuals how to master the skills necessary to live independently and often encourage them to participate in various educational or recreational programs. Specialists also serve as a source of information, referring clients to financial aid, benefits, and legal advice. These workers may be employed directly by an individual or indirectly through community planning, research, and publicity projects.

HISTORY

Helping those with disabilities has long been a part of the social work profession. As early as 1657, facilities called almshouses provided shelter, food, and work to the poor and those with disabilities. In the mid-1800s, middle-class women referred to as "friendly visitors" visited the homes of poor families to instruct the disabled in household management, the pursuit of employment, and the education of children. However, these friendly visitors and other early charitable organizations were sometimes limited in whom they would serve, often providing help and information only to those with their same moral views and religious backgrounds.

People with severe disabilities were often confined to institutions. By the late 18th century, many states and counties had built these facilities, then referred to as insane asylums, for the 24-hour care of people suffering from afflictions ranging from mental retardation to paralysis. The patients of these hospitals were often committed against their will by relatives. Few efforts were made to help patients return to society to lead normal, active lives.

The settlement houses of the late 19th century, such as Jane Addams's Hull House of Chicago, led to the development of more sensitive and enlightened ways to help people. Social workers lived among the residents, listening and learning along with them. But even with this new understanding of social work, those with disabilities were still unable to get complete assistance. Society wanted to help those in need but didn't necessarily want to live among them. As a result, separate schools, workplaces, and agencies for the disabled were established. Although social workers instructed blind people in how to cook and clean, how to use a guide dog, and how to read Braille, they made few efforts to integrate them into the community.

Legal efforts to end this discrimination began in 1920 with the passing of the Vocational Rehabilitation Act. This act led to the development of state and federal agencies focused on enhancing the employment opportunities for people with disabilities. Over the years, this act has broadened to include job counseling and retraining services and the provision of prosthetic and other assisting devices. More recent efforts toward ending discrimination in employment and public services include the passing of the Americans with Disabilities Act of 1990.

THE JOB

Although he was diagnosed with multiple sclerosis years ago, Ken Smith has only recently required the use of a wheelchair. He also has only partial use of his right hand. For the last few years, he has worked as a newspaper journalist, driving himself to crime scenes, taking notes during interviews, and writing at a frantic pace to keep up with the pace of the newsroom. Now that he requires a wheelchair to get around, he is going to have to make many adjustments in his life. Fortunately for Smith, there are a number of services and benefits to help him; he just needs to know how to find this help.

The simple act of providing information is one of the most important jobs of an orientation and mobility specialist. These workers help to direct people like Smith to the many agencies available that assist those with vision and mobility impairments. By listening carefully to the problem, orientation and mobility specialists determine the best route for assistance, contact the agency on behalf of the client, and make sure the client receives the proper assistance. Because of limited funding and support, disability services are often unable to promote themselves. The biggest problem facing communities is not the lack of services available, but the lack of public awareness of these outlets.

However, Smith will require much more than names and phone numbers from an orientation and mobility specialist. He not only needs to find the right wheelchair, but he also needs instruction on how to use it. His home must be analyzed to determine what modifications need to be made (for example, wheelchair ramps, handrails, and wider doorways). If the necessary modifications cannot be made, he will have to consider moving to a new place. For all of these somewhat daunting decisions, Smith can ask an orientation and mobility specialist for advice.

Smith's workplace may also require modifications. Though perfectly capable of continuing his work as a journalist, he is going to have to fulfill his duties in different ways. For example, a special car may be required. Because of the limited use of his hand, he may need a modified computer keyboard or an assistant. An orientation and mobility specialist can serve as a client's advocate, negotiating with employers to prevent any cause for discrimination in the workplace. Specialists may also offer training and education programs to integrate or reintegrate the client into the workplace.

An orientation and mobility specialist also serves as a counselor. A client may need individual therapy or a support group. The family of the client may also need counseling on how to adjust to a parent's or child's disability.

In addition to offering services that directly benefit the client (counseling, advocacy, education, and referral), some specialists may offer services that have indirect benefits for clients. These additional services include outreach, publicity, planning, and research. Because of a general lack of awareness of the social services available, orientation and mobility specialists may focus on ways to educate the public about the challenges facing those with disabilities. They may lead fund-raising efforts for research or programs aimed at assisting the disabled community.

REQUIREMENTS

High School

Because you will need a college degree and a well-rounded education, take your high school's program of college preparatory classes. These classes should include math and science courses as well as a foreign language. Strong communication skills are needed for this work, so to improve your skills in this area take four years of English. Speech and journalism classes are also beneficial. Courses in history, social studies, sociology, and psychology are also recommended.

Because a large part of the job is providing information about disability services, you should be comfortable using the Internet and various computer programs. Not only will you have to be able to work with computers yourself, you may be required to teach clients how to use them, too.

Postsecondary Training

The Association for Education and Rehabilitation of the Blind and Visually Impaired (commonly known as AER) provides a listing of approved orientation and mobility programs at the graduate, undergraduate, and certification-only levels. Programs include instruction in mobility techniques, where students simulate blindness or limited vision with blindfolds or other devices. Internships with disability agencies are also incorporated into the programs.

Other specialists prepare themselves for the career by studying social work. The Council on Social Work Education requires that five areas be covered in accredited bachelor's degree social work programs: human behavior and the social environment, social welfare policy and services, social work practice, research, and field practicum. Most programs require two years of liberal arts study, followed by two years of study in the social work major. Also, students must complete a field practicum of at least 400 hours.

Though some starting positions require only a bachelor's degree, most supervisory and administrative positions within social work require further education. Graduate programs are organized according to fields of practice (e.g., mental health care), problem areas (e.g., substance abuse), population groups (e.g., the elderly), and practice roles (e.g., practice with individuals, families, or communities). They are usually two-year programs with at least 900 hours of field practice. Doctoral degrees are also available for those interested in research, planning, or community outreach jobs.

Certification or Licensing

Only selected states require orientation and mobility specialists to be certified. The Academy for Certification of Vision Rehabilitation and Education Professionals offers certification for orientation and mobility specialists who meet certain educational and experience requirements. To be eligible to sit for the certification exam, individuals must first complete an AER-approved orientation and mobility program.

Other Requirements

For years, people with disabilities have faced discrimination. This discrimination is fueled by fear, by misunderstanding, and by the way people with disabilities are represented in popular culture. Orientation and mobility specialists must be able to honestly address their own perceptions of people with disabilities. Specialists must be sensitive to the client's situation and have a genuine interest in involving that person in the community and workplace.

Specialists also work frequently with the elderly, which requires understanding the aging experience. Workers must be patient and be good listeners to provide the elderly with the supportive network they need.

Communication skills are also very important. Much of the work as an orientation and mobility specialist involves talking and listening to clients, teaching, interviewing, and counseling. You will need to provide clear instructions to clients, their families, and their employers.

Because many of the problems facing those with disabilities stem from discrimination, many specialists work to educate the public about living with disabilities through research, reports, and fund-raising. Being comfortable talking to a variety of people and in a variety of settings is an asset for these specialists.

EXPLORING

To learn more about this work, you can explore websites concerning disabilities and social work. A job in the school or public library helping people conduct research will put your information retrieval skills to good use. Working on the school newspaper will also help you develop your writing, researching, and interviewing skills, all important aspects of social work.

Part-time data entry jobs at a hospital or long-term care facility can familiarize you with medical terminology and the services available to people with disabilities. A part-time job in a retail pharmacy will involve you directly with people with disabilities and also the services that pay for the rental and purchase of wheelchairs, walkers, and canes. You can also gain experience by volunteering at any social service agency to get a sense of the work environment and responsibilities.

EMPLOYERS

Orientation and mobility specialists can find work with for-profit, nonprofit, and public programs. They may work in hospitals and community agencies such as transitional living services or with private agencies that focus on providing services specifically to those with disabilities.

An orientation and mobility specialist may also be self-employed, providing service on a contract basis to individuals or social service agencies.

STARTING OUT

To gain experience in social work, consider working with a social service agency specializing in information and referral. Rehabilitation centers, senior homes, schools, and summer camps for the blind, visually impaired, and disabled also offer many opportunities for experience. Because of limited funding, staffing may consist of only a few social work professionals, and the rest may be volunteers or assistants. Volunteer work may lead to full-time employment or simply introduce you to other social work professionals who can provide career guidance and letters of reference.

ADVANCEMENT

Orientation and mobility specialists may advance to become supervisors of assistants or executive directors of rehabilitation agencies. Another possible route for advancement is through teaching.

The more challenging and better paying jobs tend to go to those with more years of practical experience and higher degrees. Further study, extensive experience, and good references will lead to advancement in the profession. Also, many social work programs offer continuing education workshops, courses, and seminars. These refresher courses help practicing specialists refine their skills and learn about new areas of practice, methods, and problems. These courses are intended to supplement previous education, not substitute for a bachelor's or master's degree. Continuing education can lead to job promotions and salary increases.

EARNINGS

The higher the degree held by specialists, the higher their earning potential. Those with a Ph.D. can take jobs in indirect service, research, and planning. Salaries also vary among regions; in general, social workers on the East and West Coasts earn higher salaries than those in the Midwest. During the first five years of practice, salaries increase faster than in later years.

Medical and public health social workers earned a median annual salary of $37,380 in 2002, according to the *Occupational Outlook Handbook*. The lowest paid 10 percent earned less than $23,840 and the highest paid 10 percent earned more than $56,320.

Specialists who work in school systems are generally paid on the same scale as teachers in the system. Those who work for private clients are usually paid by the hour or per session.

WORK ENVIRONMENT

Orientation and mobility specialists work part of the time in an office, analyzing and updating client files, interviewing clients over the phone, and talking with other service agencies. Depending on the size of the agency, office duties such as typing letters, filing, and answering phones may be performed by an aide or volunteer.

The rest of their time is spent outside the office, interacting directly with clients and others. Orientation and mobility specialists are involved directly with the people they serve and must carefully examine their clients' living conditions and family relations.

Advocacy involves work in a variety of different environments; it involves meetings with clients' employers, agency directors, and local legislators. Should the client press charges for discrimination, orientation and mobility specialists may be called upon to testify in court.

Both counseling and advocacy can be stressful aspects of the work, but helping to empower people with disabilities can be very rewarding.

OUTLOOK

According to the American Association of People with Disabilities, more than 50 million people (one out of every five Americans) have a disability. In addition to continuing the fight against discrimination in the workplace and in general society, the disabled also need assistance in order to live productive lives.

Future funding is an important consideration for social service agencies. In many cases, the agencies providing information and referral must compete for funding with the very programs to which they refer people. This calls for good relationships between agencies and services. In order for agencies to receive adequate funding, social workers, including orientation and mobility specialists, must conduct research and provide reports to federal, state, and local governments showing proof of financial need. Their reports help to illustrate where funds should be allocated to best serve the disabled community.

According to the U.S. Department of Labor, the employment of social workers, including those that work with the visually and physically impaired, is expected to increase faster than the average for all occupations through 2012. Specialists will continue to increase public awareness of the importance of aid for the disabled and visually impaired. Assistance services will continue to make their way into more public areas, such as libraries, workplaces, and other public facilities.

New computer technology will continue to cater to the special needs of the disabled. The development of specialized equipment and the expansion of Internet resources allow the disabled and visually impaired to access online resources for assistance. Orientation and mobility specialists will be needed to help those with disabilities use new technology to their best advantage.

FOR MORE INFORMATION

For information on certification and educational programs, contact the following organizations:

Academy for Certification of Vision Rehabilitation & Education Professionals
463 North 1st Avenue, #1
Tucson, AZ 85718
Tel: 520-887-6816
Email: info@acvrep.org
http://www.acvrep.org

Association for Education and Rehabilitation of the Blind and Visually Impaired
1703 North Beauregard Street, Suite 440
Alexandria, VA 22311
Tel: 703-671-4500
http://www.aerbvi.org

For resources and advocacy for the disabled community, contact

American Association of People with Disabilities
1629 K Street NW, Suite 503
Washington, DC 20006
Tel: 800-840-8844
http://www.aapd.com

To read frequently asked questions about how to become a social worker, check out the following website:
Council on Social Work Education
1725 Duke Street, Suite 500
Alexandria, VA 22314-3457
Tel: 703-683-8080
Email: info@cswe.org
http://www.cswe.org

For information about careers, education, and job leads, contact
National Association of Social Workers
750 First Street, NE, Suite 700
Washington, DC 20002-4241
Tel: 800-638-8799
Email: membership@naswdc.org
http://www.socialworkers.org

For career information and job listings available in Canada, contact
Canadian Association of Social Workers
383 Parkdale Avenue, Suite 402
Ottawa, ON K1Y 4R4
Canada
Tel: 613-729-6668
Email: casw@casw-acts.ca
http://www.casw-acts.ca

Physical Therapists

OVERVIEW

Physical therapists, formerly called *physiotherapists,* are health care specialists who restore mobility, alleviate pain and suffering, and work to prevent permanent disability for their patients. They test and measure the functions of patients' musculoskeletal, neurological, pulmonary, and cardiovascular systems and treat problems in these systems caused by illness, injury, or birth defect. Physical therapists provide preventive, restorative, and rehabilitative treatment for their patients. Approximately 137,000 physical therapists are licensed to practice in the United States.

HISTORY

The practice of physical therapy has developed as our knowledge of medicine and our understanding of the functions of the human body have grown. During the first part of the 20th century, there were tremendous strides in medical practice in general. The wartime experiences of medical teams who had to rehabilitate seriously injured soldiers contributed to the medical use and acceptance of physical therapy practices. The polio epidemic in the 1940s, which left many victims paralyzed, also led to the demand for improved physical therapy.

A professional association was organized in 1921, and physical therapy began to achieve professional stature. The American Physical Therapy Association (APTA) now serves a membership of more than 63,000 physical therapists, physical therapy assistants, and students.

Today the use of physical therapy has expanded beyond hospitals, where it has been traditionally practiced. Physical therapists now are working in private practices, nursing homes, sports facilities, home health agencies, public and private schools, academic institutions, hospices, and in industrial physical therapy programs, a reflection of their versatility of skills and the public's need for comprehensive health care.

THE JOB

To initiate a program of physical therapy, the physical therapist consults the individual's medical history, examines the patient and identifies problems, confers with the physician or other health care professionals involved in the patient's care, establishes objectives and treatment goals that are consistent with the patient's needs, and determines the methods for accomplishing the objectives.

Treatment goals established by the physical therapist include preventing disability, relieving pain, and restoring function. In the presence of illness or injury, the ultimate goal is to assist the patient's physical recovery and reentry into the community, home, and work environment at the highest level of independence and self-sufficiency possible.

To aid and maintain recovery, the physical therapist also provides education to involve patients in their own care. The educational program may include exercises, posture reeducation, and relaxation practices. In many cases, the patient's family is involved in the educational program to provide emotional support or physical assistance as needed. These activities evolve into a continuum of self-care when the patient is discharged from the physical therapy program.

Physical therapists provide care for many types of patients of all ages. This includes working with burn victims to prevent abnormal scarring and loss of movement, with stroke victims to regain movement and independent living, with cancer patients to relieve discomfort, and with cardiac patients to improve endurance and achieve independence. Physical therapists also provide preventive exercise programs, postural improvement, and physical conditioning to individuals who perceive the need to promote their own health and well-being.

Physical therapists should have a creative approach to their work. No two patients respond the same way to exactly the same kind of treatment. The challenge is to find the right way to encourage the patient to make progress, to respond to treatment, to feel a sense of achievement, and to refuse to become discouraged if progress is slow.

Many physical therapists acquire specialized knowledge through clinical experience and educational preparation in specialty areas of practice, such as cardiopulmonary physical therapy, clinical electrophysiologic physical therapy, neurologic physical therapy, orthopedic physical therapy, pediatric physical therapy, geriatric physical therapy, and sports physical therapy.

REQUIREMENTS

High School

While you are in high school you can begin to prepare for this career by taking college preparatory classes. These should include biology, chemistry, physics, health, and mathematics. Because so much of this work involves direct contact with clients, you should improve your people skills as well as your communication skills by taking psychology, sociology, and English classes. Also, take computer science courses so that you are computer literate. Statistics, history, and a foreign language are also beneficial.

Postsecondary Training

Physical therapists attain their professional skills through extensive education that takes place both in the classroom and in clinical settings. You should attend a school accredited by the Commission on Accreditation in Physical Therapy Education (CAPTE) to receive the most thorough education. CAPTE now only accredits schools offering postbaccalaureate degrees (master's and doctorate degrees), and you will need one of these degrees to practice physical therapy. Previously, CAPTE had accredited bachelor's degree programs; however, this change was made to give students an appropriate amount of time to study liberal arts as well as a physical therapy curriculum. Course work should include classes in the humanities as well as those geared for the profession, such as anatomy, human growth and development, and therapeutic procedures. Clinical experience is done as supervised fieldwork in such settings as hospitals, home care agencies, and nursing homes. According to APTA, there are 157 accredited programs offering master's degrees and 42 offering doctorates in physical therapy. Visit the APTA website (http://www.apta.org) for a listing of accredited programs.

Certification or Licensing

Specialist certification of physical therapists, while not a requirement for employment, is a desirable advanced credential. The American Board of Physical Therapy Specialties, an appointed group of the American Physical Therapy Association, certifies physical therapists who demonstrate specialized knowledge and advanced clinical proficiency in a specialty area of physical therapy practice and who pass a certifying examination. The seven areas of specialization are cardiovascular and pulmonary, clinical electrophysiology, neurology, orthopedics, pediatrics, geriatrics, and sports.

Upon graduating from an accredited physical therapy educational program, all physical therapists must successfully complete a

No two patients respond to treatments exactly the same way, so physical therapists must be creative in their approaches to each patient's needs. *(Getty Images)*

national examination. Other licensing requirements vary by state. You will need to check with the licensing board of the state in which you hope to work for specific information.

Other Requirements

Successful physical therapists enjoy working with people and helping others to feel better, both physically and emotionally. They need creativity and patience to determine a treatment plan for each client and to help them achieve treatment goals. Physical therapists must also be committed to lifelong learning because new developments in technology and medicine mean that therapists must continually update their knowledge. It is also a plus to have a positive attitude and an outgoing personality.

EXPLORING

Your first step in exploring this field could be to talk with a physical therapist in your community about the work. Your school guidance counselor should be able to help you arrange for such an informational interview. Hands-on experience is important to get because schools that you apply to will take this into consideration. This experience will also help you decide how well you like working with people who are sometimes in pain or confused. One possibility is to volunteer at a physical therapy program. If such an opening is not available, try volunteering at a local hospital, nursing home, or other care facility to gain experience working in these settings. You can also look for volunteer opportunities or summer jobs at camps for the disabled. Paid part-time positions may also be available as a hospital orderly or aide to a physical therapist.

EMPLOYERS

According to the U.S. Department of Labor, about two-thirds of physical therapists work in hospitals or in offices of other health practitioners. Physical therapists may be involved in research or teach at colleges and universities. Veterans Administration hospitals and other government agencies also hire physical therapists.

STARTING OUT

Physical therapy graduates may obtain jobs through their college placement offices or by answering ads in any of a variety of professional journals. They can apply in person or send letters and resumes to hospitals, medical centers, rehabilitation facilities, and other places that hire physical therapists. Some find jobs through the APTA.

ADVANCEMENT

In a hospital or other health care facility, one may rise from being a staff physical therapist to being the chief physical therapist and then director of the department. Administrative responsibilities are usually given to those physical therapists who have had several years of experience plus the personal qualities that prepare them for undertaking this kind of assignment.

After serving in a hospital or other institution for several years, some physical therapists open up their own practices or go into a group practice, with both often paying higher salaries.

EARNINGS

Salaries for physical therapists depend on experience and type of employer. According to the *Occupational Outlook Handbook*, physical therapists earned an annual average salary of $57,330 in 2002. Fifty percent averaged between $48,480 and $70,050; the lowest paid 10 percent earned less than $40,200, and the highest paid 10 percent earned over $86,260 a year. Physical therapists working in nursing care facilities made median salaries of $57,570, and those working for home health care services made $62,480.

WORK ENVIRONMENT

The typical physical therapist works approximately 40 hours each week, including Saturdays. Patient sessions may be brief or may last an hour or more. Usually, treatment is on an individual basis, but occasionally therapy may be given in groups when the patients' problems are similar.

OUTLOOK

The U.S. Department of Labor predicts faster than average job growth for physical therapists through 2012. The median age of the American population is rising, and this older demographic group tends to develop a higher number of medical conditions that cause physical pain and disability. Also, advances in medical technology save more people, who then require physical therapy. For example, as more trauma victims and newborns with birth defects survive, the need for physical therapists will rise. Another reason is the public's growing interest in physical fitness, which has resulted in an increasing number of athletic injuries requiring physical therapy. In industry and fitness centers, a growing interest in pain and injury prevention also has created new opportunities for physical therapists.

Employment prospects for physical therapists should continue to be excellent into the next decade. If enrollment in accredited physical therapy programs remains at the current level, there will be more openings for physical therapists than qualified individuals to fill them.

FOR MORE INFORMATION

The APTA offers the brochure A Future in Physical Therapy, *a directory of accredited schools, certification, and general career information.*

American Physical Therapy Association (APTA)
1111 North Fairfax Street
Alexandria, VA 22314-1488
Tel: 800-999-2782
http://www.apta.org

For information on accredited programs, contact
Commission on Accreditation in Physical Therapy Education
(CAPTE)
Email: accreditation@apta.org
http://www.apta.org/Education/accreditation

Recreational Therapists

OVERVIEW

Recreational therapists plan, organize, direct, and monitor medically approved recreation programs for patients in hospitals, clinics, and various community settings. These therapists use recreational activities to assist patients with mental, physical, or emotional disabilities to achieve the maximum possible functional independence. Recreational therapists hold almost 27,000 jobs in the United States.

HISTORY

The field of therapy has expanded in the past few decades to include recreational therapy as a form of medical treatment. Its use grew out of the realization that soldiers suffering from battle fatigue, shock, and emotional trauma respond positively to organized recreation and activity programs.

As a result, therapy for people in nursing homes, hospitals, mental institutions, and adult care facilities is no longer limited to physical therapy. Experiments have shown that recovery is aided by recreational activities such as sports, music, art, gardening, dance, drama, field trips, and other pastimes. Elderly people are more healthy and alert when their days are filled with activities, field trips, and social get-togethers. People with disabilities can gain greater self-confidence and awareness of their own abilities when they get involved with sports, crafts, and other activities. People recovering from drug or alcohol addiction can reaffirm their self-worth through directed hobbies, clubs, and sports. The recreational therapist is a health professional who organizes these types of activities and helps patients take an active role in their own recovery.

THE JOB

Recreational therapists work with people who are mentally, physically, or emotionally disabled. They are professionals who employ leisure activities as a form of treatment, much as other health practitioners use surgery, drugs, nutrition, exercise, or psychotherapy. Recreational therapists strive to minimize patients' symptoms, restore function, and improve their physical, mental, and emotional well-being. Enhancing the patient's ability to take part in everyday life is the primary goal of recreational therapy; interesting and rewarding activities are the means for working toward that goal.

Recreational therapists work in a number of different settings, including mental hospitals, psychiatric day hospitals, community mental health centers, nursing homes, adult day care programs, residential facilities for the mentally disabled, school systems, and prisons. They can work as individual staff members, as independent consultants, or as part of a larger therapeutic team. They may get personally involved with patients or direct the work of assistants and support staff.

The recreational therapist first confers with the doctors, psychiatrists, social workers, physical therapists, and other professionals on staff to coordinate their efforts in treatment. The recreational therapist needs to understand the nature of the patient's ailment, current physical and mental capacities, emotional state, and prospects for recovery. The patient's family and friends are also consulted to find out the patient's interests and hobbies. With this information, the recreational therapist then plans an agenda of activities for that person.

To enrich the lives of people in hospitals and other institutions, recreational therapists use imagination and skill in organizing beneficial activities. Sports, games, arts and crafts, movie screenings, field trips, hobby clubs, and dramatics are only a few examples of activities that can enrich the lives of patients. Some therapists specialize in certain areas. *Dance/movement therapists* plan and conduct dance and body movement exercises to improve patients' physical and mental well-being. *Art therapists* work with patients in various art methods, such as drawing, painting, and ceramics, as part of their therapeutic and recovery programs. Therapists may also work with pets and other animals, such as horses. *Music therapists* design programs for patients that can involve solo or group singing, playing in bands, rhythmic and other creative activities, listening to music, or attending concerts. Even flowers and gardening can prove beneficial to patients, as is proved by the work of *horticultural therapists*. When the treatment team feels that regular employment would help certain patients, the *industrial therapist* arranges a productive job for the patient in an actual work environment, one that will have the greatest therapeutic value based on the patient's needs and abilities. *Orientation therapists* for the blind work with people who have recently lost their sight, helping them to readjust to daily living and independence through training and exercise. All of these professional therapists plan their programs to meet the needs and capabilities of patients. They also carefully monitor and record each patient's progress and report it to the other members of the medical team.

As part of their jobs, recreational therapists need to understand their patients and set goals for their progress accordingly. A patient having trouble socializing, for example, may have an interest in playing chess but be overwhelmed by the prospect of actually playing, since that involves interaction with another person. A therapist would proceed slowly, first letting the patient observe a number of games and then assigning a therapeutic assistant to serve as a chess partner for weeks or even months, as long as it takes for the patient to gain enough confidence to seek out other patients for chess partners. The therapist makes a note of the patient's response, modifies the therapy program accordingly, and lets other professionals know of the results. If a patient responds more enthusiastically to the program, works more cooperatively with others, or becomes more disruptive, the therapist must note these reactions and periodically reevaluate the patient's activity program.

Responsibilities and elements of the job can vary, depending on the setting in which the recreational therapist works. In nursing homes, the therapist often groups residents according to common or shared interests and ability levels and then plans field trips, parties, entertainment, and other group activities. The therapist documents residents' responses to the activities and continually searches for ways of heightening residents' enjoyment of recreational and leisure activities, not just in the facility but in the surrounding community as well. Because nursing home residents are likely to remain in the facility for months or even years, the activities program makes a big difference in the quality of their lives. Without the stimulation of interesting events to look forward to and participate in, the daily routine of a nursing home can become monotonous and depressing, and some residents are apt to deteriorate both mentally and physically. In some nursing homes, recreational therapists direct the activities program.

In others, *activities coordinators* plan and carry out the program under the part-time supervision of a consultant who is either a recreational or occupational therapist.

The therapist in a community center might work in a day-care program for the elderly or in a program for mentally disabled adults operated by a county recreation department. No matter what the disability, recreational therapists in community settings face the added logistical challenge of arranging transportation and escort services, if necessary, for prospective participants. Coordinating transportation is less of a problem in hospitals and nursing homes, where the patients all live under one roof. Developing therapeutic recreation programs in community settings requires a large measure of organizational ability, flexibility, and ingenuity.

Recreational therapy is a relatively new field, but it is already a respected, integral part of the treatment of many elderly and disabled people. Clients often need extra encouragement and support to stay active and build on the things they can, rather than can't, do. The activity programs that recreational therapists design and operate can add immeasurable enjoyment to the lives of patients. Beyond this, the activities provide opportunities for exercise and social interaction and may also help relieve anxiety and loneliness, build confidence, and promote each patient's independence.

REQUIREMENTS

High School
You can prepare for a career as a recreational therapist by taking your high school's college preparatory program. Naturally, this should include science classes, such as biology and chemistry, as well as mathematics and history classes. You can begin to gain an understanding of human behavior by taking psychology and sociology classes. For exposure to a variety of recreation specialties, take physical education, art, music, and drama classes. Verbal and written communication skills are essential for this work, so take English and speech classes. This job will require you to write reports, so computer science skills are also essential.

Postsecondary Training
Approximately 140 recreational therapy programs, which offer degrees ranging from the associate to the doctoral level, are currently available in the United States. While associate degrees in recreational therapy exist, such a degree will allow you only to work at the paraprofessional level. To be eligible for an entry-level professional

position as a recreational therapist, you will need a bachelor's degree. Acceptable majors are recreational therapy, therapeutic recreation, and recreation with a concentration in therapeutic recreation. A typical four-year bachelor's degree program includes courses in both natural science (such as biology, behavioral science, and human anatomy) and social science (such as psychology and sociology). Courses more specific to the profession include programming for special populations; rehabilitative techniques including self-help skills, mobility, signing for the deaf, and orientation for the blind; medical equipment; current treatment approaches; legal issues; and professional ethics. In addition, you will need to complete a supervised internship or field placement lasting a minimum of 480 hours.

Continuing education is increasingly becoming a requirement for professionals in this field. Many therapists attend conferences and seminars and take additional university courses. A number of professional organizations (for example, the National Therapeutic Recreation Society, the American Therapeutic Recreation Association, and the American Alliance for Health, Physical Education, Recreation, and Dance) offer continuing education opportunities. Those with degrees in related fields can enter the profession by earning master's degrees in therapeutic recreation. Advanced degrees are recommended for those seeking advancement to supervisory, administrative, and teaching positions. These requirements will become more strict as more professionals enter the field.

Certification or Licensing

A number of states regulate the profession of therapeutic recreation. Licensing is required in some states; professional certification (or eligibility for certification) is required in others; titling is regulated in some states and at some facilities. In other states, many hospitals and other employers require recreational therapists to be certified. Certification is recommended for recreational therapists as a way to show professional accomplishment. It is available through the National Council for Therapeutic Recreation Certification. To receive certification you must meet eligibility requirements, including education and experience, as well as pass an exam. You are then given the title certified therapeutic recreation specialist (CTRS). Because of the variety of certification and licensing requirements, you must check with both your state and your employer for specific information on your situation.

Other Requirements

To be a successful recreational therapist, you must enjoy and be enthusiastic about the activities in which you involve your clients. You will also need patience and a positive attitude. Since this is people-oriented work, therapists must be able to relate to many different people in a variety of settings. They must be able to deal assertively and politely with other health care workers, such as doctors and nurses, as well as with the clients themselves and their families. In addition, successful therapists must be creative and have strong communication skills in order to develop and explain activities to patients.

EXPLORING

If you are interested in recreational therapy, you can find part-time or summer work as a sports coach or referee, park supervisor, or camp counselor. Volunteer work in a nursing home, hospital, or care facility for disabled adults is also a good way to learn about the daily realities of institutional living. These types of facilities are always looking for volunteers to work with and visit patients. Working with people with physical, mental, or emotional disabilities can be stressful, and volunteer work is a good way for you to test whether you can handle this kind of stress.

EMPLOYERS

Recreational therapists hold almost 27,000 jobs, according to the U.S. Department of Labor. About one-third of these jobs are in nursing and personal care facilities and one-third are in hospitals. Other employers include residential facilities, adult day care centers, and substance abuse centers, and some therapists are self-employed. Employment opportunities also exist in long-term rehabilitation, home health care, correctional facilities, psychiatric facilities, and transitional programs.

STARTING OUT

There are many methods for finding out about available jobs in recreational therapy. A good place to start is the job notices and want ads printed in the local newspapers, bulletins from state park and recreation societies, and publications of the professional associations previously mentioned. State employment agencies and human service departments will know of job openings in state hospitals. College placement offices might also be able to put new recreational therapy graduates in touch with prospective employers. Internship programs are sometimes available, offering good opportunities to find potential full-time jobs.

Recent graduates should also make appointments to meet potential employers personally. Most colleges and universities offer career

Books to Read

Austin, David R.. *Therapeutic Recreation: Processes and Techniques.*
5th ed. Champaign, Ill.: Sagamore Publishing, 2003.

Cheshire, Nancy, and Martha Kenney. *Everything from A to Y: The
Zest is up to You! Older Adult Activities for Every Day of the Year.*
State College, Pa.: Venture, 1999.

Dattilo, John. *Facilitation Techniques in Therapeutic Recreation.* State
College, Pa.: Venture, 2000.

Wilhite, Barbara, and Jean Keller. *Therapeutic Recreation: Cases and
Exercises.* 2nd ed. State College, Pa.: Venture, 2001.

counseling services. Most employers will make themselves available
to discuss their programs and the possibility of hiring extra staff. They
may also guide new graduates to other institutions currently hiring
therapists. Joining professional associations, both state and national, and attending conferences are good ways to meet potential
employers and colleagues.

ADVANCEMENT

Newly graduated recreational therapists generally begin as staff therapists. Advancement is chiefly to supervisory or administrative positions, usually after some years of experience and continuing
education. Some therapists teach, conduct research, or do consulting
work on a contract basis; a graduate degree is essential for moving
into these areas.

Many therapists continue their education but prefer to continue
working with patients. For variety, they may choose to work with
new groups of people or get a job in a new setting, such as moving
from a retirement home to a facility for the disabled. Some may also
move to a related field, such as special education, or sales positions
involving products and services related to recreational therapy.

EARNINGS

Salaries of recreational therapists vary according to educational
background, experience, certification, and region of the country.
Recreational therapists had median earnings of $30,540 in 2002,

according to the U.S. Department of Labor. The lowest paid 10 percent earned less than $18,130 a year, while the highest paid 10 percent earned more than $47,180 annually. Employment setting is also an important factor in determining salary. Recreational therapists employed by personal care agencies and nursing facilities earned median incomes of $25,010. Those in management positions command higher salaries. Supervisors report top salaries of $50,000 per year; administrators reported maximum earnings of $65,000 annually; and some consultants and educators reported even higher earnings.

Therapists employed at hospitals, clinics, and other facilities generally enjoy a full benefits package, including health insurance and vacation, holiday, and sick pay. Consultants and self-employed therapists must provide their own benefits.

WORK ENVIRONMENT

Working conditions vary, but recreational therapists generally work in a ward, a specially equipped activity room, or at a nursing home. In a community setting, recreational therapists may interview subjects and plan activities in an office, but they might work in a gymnasium, swimming pool, playground, or outdoors on a nature walk when leading activities. Therapists may also work on horse ranches, farms, and other outdoor facilities catering to people with disabilities.

The job may be physically tiring because therapists are often on their feet all day and may have to lift and carry equipment. Recreational therapists generally work a standard 40-hour week, although weekend and evening hours may be required. Supervisors may have to work overtime, depending on their workload.

OUTLOOK

The U.S. Department of Labor predicts that employment for recreational therapists will grow more slowly than the average through 2012. Employment in nursing homes will grow slightly faster than in other areas. Fast employment growth is expected in assisted living, outpatient physical and psychiatric rehabilitation, and services for people with disabilities. Increased life expectancies of the elderly and people with developmental disabilities, such as Down's Syndrome, will create opportunities for recreational therapists. The incidence of alcohol and drug dependency problems is also growing, creating a demand for qualified therapists to work in short-term alcohol and drug abuse clinics.

Most openings for recreational therapists will be in health care and assisted living facilities because of the increasing numbers and greater longevity of the elderly. There is also greater public pressure to regulate and improve the quality of life in retirement centers, which may mean more jobs and increased scrutiny of recreational therapists.

Growth in hospital jobs is not expected to be great. Many of the new jobs created will be in hospital-based adult day care programs or in units offering short-term mental health services. Because of economic and social factors, no growth is expected in public mental hospitals. Many of the programs and services formerly offered there are being shifted to community residential facilities for the disabled. Community programs for special populations are expected to expand significantly.

FOR MORE INFORMATION

For career information and resources, contact
American Association for Leisure and Recreation
1900 Association Drive
Reston, VA 20191
Tel: 800-213-7193, ext. 472
Email: aalr@aahperd.org
http://www.aahperd.org/aalr

For career information, a list of colleges and universities that offer training, and job listings, contact
American Therapeutic Recreation Association
1414 Prince Street, Suite 204
Alexandria, VA 22314
Tel: 703-683-9420
Email: atra@atra-tr.org
http://www.atra-tr.org

For information on certification, contact
National Council for Therapeutic Recreation Certification
7 Elmwood Drive
New City, NY 10956
Tel: 845-639-1439
Email: nctrc@nctrc.org
http://www.nctrc.org

For career information, visit the NTRS under Branches on the website of the National Recreation and Park Association.

National Therapeutic Recreation Society (NTRS)
22377 Belmont Ridge Road
Ashburn, VA 20148
Tel: 703-858-0784
Email: ntrsnrpa@nrpa.org
http://www.nrpa.org

Visit this website to find out about jobs, activities, schools, and other information related to the field.

Therapeutic Recreation Directory
http://www.recreationtherapy.com

Rehabilitation Counselors

QUICK FACTS

School Subjects
Psychology
Sociology

Personal Skills
Helping/teaching
Technical/scientific

Work Environment
Primarily indoors
Primarily one location

Minimum Education Level
Bachelor's degree

Salary Range
$16,840 to $25,840 to
$44,940+

Certification or Licensing
Recommended

Outlook
Faster than the average

DOT
045

GOE
10.01.02

NOC
4153

O*NET-SOC
21-1015.00

OVERVIEW

Rehabilitation counselors provide counseling and guidance services to people with disabilities to help them resolve life problems and to train for and locate work that is suitable to their physical and mental abilities, interests, and aptitudes. There are approximately 122,000 rehabilitation counselors working in the United States.

HISTORY

Today it is generally accepted that people with disabilities can and should have the opportunity to become as fully independent as possible in all aspects of life, from school to work to social activities. In response to the needs of disabled war veterans, Congress passed the first Vocational Rehabilitation Act in 1920. The act set in place the Vocational Rehabilitation Program, a federal-state program that provides for the delivery of rehabilitation services, including counseling, to eligible people with disabilities.

The profession of rehabilitation counseling has its roots in the Rehabilitation Act, which allowed for funds to train personnel. What was at first a job title developed into a fully recognized profession as it became evident that the delivery of effective rehabilitation services required highly trained specialists. Early efforts for providing rehabilitation counseling and other services were often directed especially toward the nation's veterans. In 1930, the Veterans Administration was created to supply support services to veterans and their families, and in 1989, the U.S. Department of Veterans Affairs was created as the 14th cabinet department in the U.S. government.

The passage of the Americans with Disabilities Act in 1990 recognized the rights and needs of people with disabilities and developed federal regulations and guidelines aimed at eliminating discrimination and other barriers preventing people with disabilities from participating fully in school, workplace, and public life. Many state and federal programs have since been created to aid people with disabilities.

THE JOB

Rehabilitation counselors work with people with disabilities to identify barriers to medical, psychological, personal, social, and vocational functioning and to develop a plan of action to remove or reduce those barriers.

Clients are referred to rehabilitation programs from many sources. Sometimes they seek help on their own initiative; sometimes their families bring them in. They may be referred by a physician, hospital, or social worker, or they may be sent by employment agencies, schools, or accident commissions. A former employer may seek help for the individual.

The counselor's first step is to determine the nature and extent of the disability and evaluate how that disability interferes with work and other life functions. This determination is made from medical and psychological reports as well as from family history, educational background, work experience, and other evaluative information.

The next step is to determine a vocational direction and plan of services to overcome the handicaps to employment or independent living.

The rehabilitation counselor coordinates a comprehensive evaluation of a client's physical functioning abilities and vocational interests, aptitudes, and skills. This information is used to develop for the client a vocational or independent-living goal and the services necessary to reach that goal. Services that the rehabilitation counselor may coordinate or provide include physical and mental restoration, academic or vocational training, vocational counseling, job analysis, job modification or reasonable accommodation, and job placement. Limited financial assistance in the form of maintenance or transportation assistance may also be provided.

The counselor's relationship with the client may be as brief as a week or as long as several years, depending on the nature of the problem and the needs of the client.

REQUIREMENTS

High School

To prepare for becoming a rehabilitation counselor, take your high school's college prep curriculum. These classes should include several years of mathematics and science, such as biology and chemistry. To begin to gain an understanding of people and societies, take history, psychology, and sociology classes. English classes are important to take because you will need excellent communication skills for this work. Some of your professional responsibilities will include documenting your work and doing research to provide your clients with helpful information; to do these things you will undoubtedly be working with computers. Therefore, you should take computer science classes so that you are skilled in using this tool. In addition, you may want to consider taking speech and a foreign language, both of which, again, will enhance your communication skills.

Postsecondary Training

Although some positions are available for people with a bachelor's degree in rehabilitation counseling, these positions are usually as aides and offer limited advancement opportunities. Most employers require the rehabilitation counselors working for them to hold master's degrees. Before receiving your master's, you will need to complete a bachelor's degree with a major in behavioral sciences, social sciences, or a related field. Another option is to complete an undergraduate degree in rehabilitation counseling. The Council for Accreditation of Counseling and Related Educational Programs (CACREP) has accredited 176 institutions that offer programs in counselor education. If you decide on an undergraduate degree in rehabilitation, it is recommended you attend an accredited program. Keep in mind, however, that even if you get an undergraduate degree in rehabilitation, you will still need to attend a graduate program to qualify for most counselor positions. No matter which undergraduate program you decide on, you should concentrate on courses in sociology, psychology, physiology, history, and statistics as well as courses in English and communications. Several universities now offer courses in various aspects of physical therapy and special education training. Courses in sign language, speech therapy, and a foreign language are also beneficial.

More than 80 graduate programs in rehabilitation counseling have been accredited by the Council on Rehabilitation Education (CORE), and to receive the most thorough education, it is recommended you attend one of these. A typical master's program usually lasts two years. Studies include courses in medical aspects of disability, psychosocial aspects of disability, testing techniques, statistics, personality theory, personality development, abnormal psychology, techniques of counseling, occupational information, and vocational training and job placement. A supervised internship is also an important aspect of a program.

Certification or Licensing

The regulation of counselors is required in 47 states and the District of Columbia. This regulation may be in the form of credentialing, registry, certification, or licensure. Regulations, however, vary by state and sometimes by employer. For example, an employer may require certification even if the state does not. You will need to check with your state's licensing board as well as your employer for specific information about your circumstances.

Across the country, many employers now require their rehabilitation counselors to be certified by the Commission on Rehabilitation Counselor Certification (CRCC). The purpose of certification is to provide assurance that professionals engaged in rehabilitation counseling meet set standards and maintain those standards through continuing education. To become certified, counselors must pass an extensive written examination to demonstrate their knowledge of rehabilitation counseling. The CRCC requires the master's degree as the minimum educational level for certification. Applicants who meet these certification requirements receive the designation certified rehabilitation counselor (CRC).

Most state government rehabilitation agencies require future counselors to meet state civil service and merit system regulations. The applicant must take a competitive written examination and may also be interviewed and evaluated by a special board.

Other Requirements

The most important personal attribute required for rehabilitation counseling is the ability to get along well with other people. Rehabilitation counselors work with many different kinds of clients and must be able to see situations and problems from the client's point of view. They must be both patient and persistent. Rehabilitation may be a slow process with many delays and setbacks. The counselor must maintain a calm, positive manner even when no progress is made.

EXPLORING

To explore a career in which you work with people with disabilities, you should look for opportunities to volunteer or work in this field.

One possibility is to be a counselor at a children's camp for disabled youngsters. You can also volunteer with a local vocational rehabilitation agency or a facility such as the Easter Seal Society or Goodwill. Other possibilities include reading for the blind or leading a hobby or craft class at an adult day care center. And don't forget volunteer opportunities at a local hospital or nursing home. Even if your only responsibility is to escort people to the X-ray department or talk to patients to cheer them up, you will gain valuable experience interacting with people who are facing challenging situations.

EMPLOYERS

Rehabilitation counselors work in a variety of settings. About three-quarters of rehabilitation counselors work for state agencies; some also work for local and federal agencies. Employment opportunities are available in rehabilitation centers, mental health agencies, developmental disability agencies, sheltered workshops, training institutions, and special schools.

STARTING OUT

School placement offices are the best places for the new graduate to begin the career search. In addition, the National Rehabilitation Counseling Association and the American Rehabilitation Counseling Association (a division of the American Counseling Association) are sources for employment information. The new counselor may also apply directly to agencies for available positions. State and local vocational rehabilitation agencies employ about 10,000 rehabilitation counselors. The Department of Veterans Affairs employs several hundred people to assist with the rehabilitation of disabled veterans. Many rehabilitation counselors are employed by private for-profit or nonprofit rehabilitation programs and facilities. Others are employed in industry, schools, hospitals, and other settings, while others are self-employed.

ADVANCEMENT

The rehabilitation counselor usually receives regular salary increases after gaining experience in the job. He or she may move from relatively easy cases to increasingly challenging ones. Counselors may advance into such positions as administrator or supervisor after several years of counseling experience. It is also possible to find related counseling and teaching positions, which may represent an advancement in other fields.

EARNINGS

The U.S. Department of Labor reports that median annual earnings of rehabilitation counselors in 2002 were $25,840. Salaries ranged from less than $16,840 to more than $42,790. Those who worked in state governments earned median incomes of $44,940.

Rehabilitation counselors employed by the federal government generally start at the GS-9 or GS-11 level. In 2004, basic GS-9 salary was $36,478. Those with master's degrees generally began at the GS-11 level, with a salary of $44,136 in 2004. Salaries for federal government workers vary according to the region of the country in which they work. Those working in areas with a higher cost of living receive additional locality pay.

Counselors employed by government and private agencies and institutions generally receive health insurance, pension plans, and other benefits, including vacation, sick, and holiday pay. Self-employed counselors must provide their own benefits.

WORK ENVIRONMENT

Rehabilitation counselors work approximately 40 hours each week and do not usually have to work during evenings or weekends. They work both in the office and in the field. Depending on the type of training required, lab space and workout or therapy rooms may be available. Rehabilitation counselors must usually keep detailed accounts of their progress with clients and write reports. They may spend many hours traveling about the community to visit employed clients, prospective employers, trainees, or training programs.

OUTLOOK

The passage of the Americans with Disabilities Act of 1990 has increased the demand for rehabilitation counselors. As more local, state, and federal programs are initiated that are designed to assist people with disabilities and as private institutions and companies seek to comply with this new legislation, job prospects are promising. Budget pressures may serve to limit the number of new rehabilitation counselors to be hired by government agencies; however, the overall outlook remains excellent.

The U.S. Department of Labor predicts that employment growth for all counselors will be faster than average through 2012. Some of this growth can be attributed to the advances in medical technology that are saving more lives. In addition, more employers are offering employee assistance programs that provide mental health and alcohol and drug abuse services.

FOR MORE INFORMATION

For general information on careers in rehabilitation counseling, contact
American Rehabilitation Counseling Association
5999 Stevenson Avenue
Alexandria, VA 22304-3300
Tel: 800-545-2223
http://www.nchrtm.okstate.edu/arca

For information on certification, contact
Commission on Rehabilitation Counselor Certification
1835 Rohlwing Road, Suite E
Rolling Meadows, IL 60008
Tel: 847-394-2104
http://www.crccertification.com

For listings of CORE-approved programs as well as other information, contact
Council on Rehabilitation Education (CORE)
1835 Rohlwing Road, Suite E
Rolling Meadows, IL 60008
Tel: 847-394-1785
http://www.core-rehab.org

To learn about government legislation, visit NRA's website.
National Rehabilitation Association (NRA)
633 South Washington Street
Alexandria, VA 22314
Tel: 703-836-0850
Email: info@nationalrehab.org
http://www.nationalrehab.org

The NRCA is a division of the National Rehabilitation Association.
For news on legislation, employment, and other information, contact
National Rehabilitation Counseling Association (NRCA)
8807 Sudley Road, Suite 102
Manassas, VA 22110-4719
Tel: 703-361-2077
Email: NRCAOFFICE@aol.com
http://nrca-net.org

For information on a variety of resources, contact
National Clearinghouse of Rehabilitation Training Materials
Oklahoma State University
206 West Sixth Street
Stillwater, OK 74078-4080
Tel: 800-223-5219
http://www.nchrtm.okstate.edu

Senior Care Pharmacists

OVERVIEW

Pharmacists are health care professionals responsible for the dispensation of prescription and nonprescription medications. They may advise physicians, nurses, or other health care professionals on the use of medications, and they also give patients instructions for taking and storing medicines. *Senior care pharmacists* have expert knowledge regarding the medical conditions of the elderly and the treatments for these conditions. Many factors must be considered when treating the elderly, making this a complicated process. One factor to keep in mind is that older bodies react differently to medications than younger bodies. In addition, many older people have more than one health problem and take more than one medication. According to the American Society of Consultant Pharmacists, people age 65–69 take an average of about 14 prescriptions a year, and as people get older the number only increases. Because of factors such as these, senior care pharmacists work closely with other members of the health care team in caring for a patient. Senior care pharmacists' responsibilities include keeping records on their patients' drug regimens, advising health professionals on what medicines to use and giving training on how to use them, and monitoring patients' progress and adjusting medicines as needed.

HISTORY

The title of pharmacist can be traced to ancient Greece. During the time of Aristotle, those who compounded drugs were called *phar-*

makons. The word has changed little from its original form and still means approximately the same thing: one who compounds drugs, medicines, or poisons.

Pharmacy as a profession grew slowly in the United States. It is said that one of the first American pharmacists was Governor John Winthrop of the Massachusetts Bay Colony. He learned to compound drugs because there were no other sources in the colony for obtaining medicines. The first school established to teach pharmacy in this country was the Philadelphia College of Pharmacy, founded in 1822. It is still in operation today as a college of the University of the Sciences in Philadelphia.

In 1906, the Federal Pure Food and Drug Act was passed. The Food and Drug Administration (FDA) was created in 1931. This agency must approve any pharmaceutical before it can be offered for sale in the United States. The field of pharmacy continued to grow, but it was only later in the 20th century that geriatric pharmacy as a profession came into existence. By the 1950s, some pharmacists had begun to focus on providing pharmacy services to nursing homes. Government health official George Archambault, now known as the founding father of this profession, coined the term *consultant pharmacist* to refer to the pharmacists working (that is, consulting) with nursing homes.

Today, senior care pharmacists, as the consultant pharmacists became known, still provide pharmacy services to nursing facilities. In addition, senior care pharmacists may provide services for elderly people in other environments, such as assisted living facilities, hospices, and home-based care programs. Because our country has a large and growing senior population, the skills and expertise of senior care pharmacists should be increasingly in demand.

THE JOB

Senior care pharmacists have expert knowledge of drug products and their effects on the elderly, the medical conditions of the elderly, and the treatments for these conditions. They work in a variety of settings, and their responsibilities vary based on the places of work. In general, however, senior care pharmacists' duties involve consulting with nursing facilities or other long-term care facilities (such as assisted living facilities, hospices, and home-based care programs) about the condition and care of their patients. These pharmacists do on-site visits to meet with their patients, discuss any problems they may be having as well as to discuss a treatment plan, and meet with the other health care professionals who are part of a team caring for the patient.

An important aspect of the senior care pharmacist's work is to conduct regular drug regimen reviews as required by law. For these reviews, senior care pharmacists gather and review information on a patient's medical history, diagnosis, test results, and treatments. In general, they go over any information related to the person's health, including his or her diet. The pharmacist also meets with the patient's doctors, nurses, and any other health professional involved in the patient's care to review treatment plans and goals. Senior care pharmacists then go over the medications prescribed for the patient, checking to make sure the patients are receiving the right medicines, in the right doses, and at the right times. If the senior care pharmacist discovers a problem with a medication being given, he or she figures out how to correct the situation.

Some of the unique knowledge senior care pharmacists have includes knowing how a medicine will affect an older person's body, knowing how different medicines will react together in clients who take more than one prescription, knowing if a medication will make an elderly person's existing conditions worse, and, just as important, knowing the life circumstances of the patient. That is, the pharmacist should know the answer to questions such as: Is someone available to give the medication to the patient on a regular basis? Or, if the patient is in an assisted living facility, will he or she remember to take the medicine? Is the patient skipping doses to make a prescription last longer? Can the patient read the instruction label? Does the patient still need the medicine, or has he or she recovered from the illness the medicine was treating? Senior care pharmacists need to be aware of all such factors in order to find appropriate solutions to any problems that may arise.

In addition to having a close relationship with other health care professionals, senior care pharmacists must have close relationships with their clients, treating each as an individual. Because an older person's body processes medication differently than a younger person's, senior care pharmacists must be able to customize medications for their patients so that they achieve the desired results. A pharmacist may suggest, for example, taking two doses of a medicine at different times during the day instead of one large dose that is more difficult for an older person's body to absorb. Many older people regularly take more than one type of drug for a variety of problems. And senior care pharmacists must know when 70-year-old Mr. Jones, for example, comes in with a prescription for a new arthritis medicine if this medicine will interfere with the effectiveness of the blood pressure medicine he is already taking. If the potential for negative drug interaction exists, the pharmacist will consult with the doctor and suggest a more appropriate treatment.

Senior care pharmacists must also understand a patient's overall health condition. Many older people, for example, have a poor sense of balance, limited vision, or are forgetful. Senior care pharmacists must know if a patient experiences any such problems so that they do not give a medicine that will make the situation worse. For example, if 82-year-old Ms. Braun (who has osteoporosis and is unsteady walking) has a prescription for a medicine that has the side effect of causing dizziness, the pharmacist should realize this might aggravate her balance problem and lead to a fall that could cause broken bones. In such a case, the senior care pharmacist will advise Ms. Braun's doctor about the problem and recommend a different medication.

Senior care pharmacists also keep detailed records of drugs dispensed to each client. This is extremely important because older people often see more than one doctor for a number of different conditions. The senior care pharmacist may be the only person keeping track of various medicines prescribed by several doctors for one patient. In these cases, the senior care pharmacist is the health care professional who is in the best position to spot a potential adverse drug interaction and recommend a prescription change.

Another responsibility of senior care pharmacists is to answer questions about medications and provide training to other health care workers on how to administer these medications. A senior care pharmacist may spend part of a day or a whole day, for example, giving nurses at a nursing home instruction on how to figure out the proper dose of an antibiotic that will be given through an IV. Naturally, senior care pharmacists also spend time in the pharmacy, where their activities include reviewing and documenting incoming prescriptions, supervising pharmacy technicians, checking filled prescriptions for their correctness, and answering questions about medications.

Like all pharmacists, senior care pharmacists must be diligent in maintaining clean and ordered work areas. They must be exceedingly accurate and precise in their calculations, and possess a high degree of concentration in order to reduce the risk of error as they assemble prescriptions. They also must be proficient with a variety of technical devices and computer systems. In conjunction with these duties, senior care pharmacists need to complete continuing education on a regular basis to maintain their certification or licensing, as required by their states. Continuing education may be done through correspondence (written responses to educational material, usually done online) or by attending conferences, workshops, and seminars. Some states may also require continuing education in particular disease topics and treatments.

Senior care pharmacists often discuss their clients' medications with them, alerting them to any harmful side effects and interactions. *(Getty Images)*

REQUIREMENTS

High School

You can start preparing for this career while you are in high school. Begin by taking a college preparatory curriculum. Be sure to take four years of math courses, including algebra, geometry, and trigonometry, and four years of science, including biology, chemistry, and physics. Take computer science classes so that you are comfortable working with computers and English classes to develop your research and writing skills. You may also want to take business classes to learn management skills and business basics. Other courses you should take include history, government, a foreign language, and a social science, such as psychology.

Postsecondary Training

The Accreditation Council for Pharmacy Education is the accrediting agency for professional programs in pharmacy offering the degree doctor of pharmacy (Pharm.D.). In the past, this agency also accredited programs that offered bachelor of science degrees in pharmacy (B.Pharm.). However, as of 2005 the Pharm.D. degree replaces the B.Pharm. degree, and all bachelor's programs in this field are being terminated. So, if you want to become a pharmacist, you should plan on getting the doctorate degree, which generally takes six years to complete.

Your first year or two of study does not take place in a school of pharmacy but rather in a general college setting where you will complete pre-pharmacy classes. Studies typically include chemistry, organic chemistry, biology, physics, calculus, statistics, anatomy, English, and social science classes, such as psychology or sociology. After completing this undergraduate work, you will need to gain admission to a school of pharmacy. If you are attending a large university that has a school of pharmacy, you may want to apply there. You may also apply for admission to schools of pharmacy that are not part of your undergraduate school. In addition to completing pre-pharmacy course work, some pharmacy schools require applicants to take the Pharmacy College Admissions Test (P-CAT) to be considered for admission.

Once you are in pharmacy school, you will take courses such as the principles of pharmacology, biochemistry, pharmacy law and ethics, and pharmaceutical care. Because geriatric pharmacy is a growing field, more and more schools are offering courses with a focus on the elderly and their pharmaceutical care needs. In addition, your education should include an internship, sometimes known as a clerkship, in which you work under the supervision of a professional pharmacist. When deciding on a school to attend, it is advisable that you consult the Accreditation Council for Pharmacy Education's Annual Directory of Accredited Professional Programs of Colleges and Schools of Pharmacy. Paper copies of this directory are available (at no charge) from the council, and directory information is also available on the council's website, http://www.acpe-accredit.org.

Certification or Licensing

The Commission for Certification in Geriatric Pharmacy offers voluntary certification to pharmacists who serve geriatric populations. To become certified, pharmacists must take a written exam that focuses on geriatric pharmacy practice. Those who pass receive the designation certified geriatric pharmacist (CGP). While this is a voluntary certification, professionals in the field highly recommend obtaining it as a demonstration of your specialized skills and knowledge.

All 50 states, the District of Columbia, and U.S. territories require practicing pharmacists to be licensed. To become licensed, candidates must have graduated from an accredited pharmacy program, completed an internship under a licensed pharmacist, and passed their state's board examination.

Other Requirements

Naturally, senior care pharmacists need to be detail-oriented as well as organized. They also need strong communication and people skills since they interact with doctors, nurses, other health professionals, elderly people who are ill, and sometimes an elderly person's family as well. They must be able to work professionally and often patiently when explaining what a medicine will do, how to take it, when to take it, and so on. Senior care pharmacists should also enjoy being around older people and want to help them. These pharmacists must be committed to a lifetime of learning because the fields of medicine and technology continue to grow, making new treatments and new methods of treatment available.

EXPLORING

One way to learn more about this profession is to read publications and visit websites dedicated to geriatric pharmacy. (You can start with the organizations' sites listed at the end of this article.) Another option is to get experience in a pharmacy environment by finding part-time or summer work at a drugstore. Even if you aren't working in the pharmacy, you can get valuable experience dealing with customers and observing the kind of work pharmacists do. If you are a hard worker and demonstrate responsibility, you may be given the chance to assist in the pharmacy, such as entering data in customer computer records, taking inventory on pharmaceuticals, bottles, and vials, preparing labels, or making deliveries to customers. Part-time or summer work in a nutrition and vitamin store can also give you the opportunity to learn a great deal about dietary supplements and herbal alternatives to pharmaceuticals.

It is also important that you explore how much you enjoy working with the elderly. Part-time or summer work in a nursing home is one way of doing this. In addition, many volunteer opportunities exist for helping older people. These opportunities can be found with organizations and agencies such as the American Red Cross, states' departments of aging, and local Catholic Charities agencies, to name a few. You will benefit from getting involved with helping older people, because you will begin to learn about their particular concerns and needs.

EMPLOYERS

Senior care pharmacists traditionally work for nursing home facilities. According to the American Society of Consultant Pharmacists, a number of employers exist within this setting. For example, a senior care pharmacist may work for a small long-term care provider, which provides pharmacy services to several nursing facilities in a small area. A senior care pharmacist can also work for a large long-term care provider, which is a pharmacy providing services to a large number of nursing facilities in a region. A pharmacist in geriatric care can also be hospital-based, working in a hospital's pharmacy and providing services to nursing facilities that are owned or run by the hospital.

There are also a growing number of senior care pharmacists employed in nontraditional settings. These pharmacists may provide services to employers such as assisted living facilities, hospice agencies, and home health programs. In addition, senior care pharmacists may be academically based, teaching at schools of pharmacy; may work in industry for drug companies as administrators or researchers; or may be self-employed, running their own consulting businesses and working with care providers such as nursing facilities, geriatric care managers, and hospice agencies.

The American Society of Consultant Pharmacists, which is the leading organization for those involved in geriatric pharmacy, reports a membership of more than 7,000. While membership is voluntary, this figure gives an idea of the number of pharmacists involved in the field.

STARTING OUT

Ward Lenart, a certified geriatric pharmacist in Chicago, Illinois, says of his career path, "I started . . . in a retail pharmacy located in a neighborhood with many geriatric customers. One day at work I noticed a customer sitting on a bench as her caregiver yelled at her, 'You need to go into a nursing home!' and 'You can't take care of yourself!' I thought to myself that there had to be more I could do [to help] . . . . I made a career change when an opportunity opened at a long-term care pharmacy. After only a few days I realized this was the type of work I went to school for." Those in geriatric pharmacy often cite the desire to provide in-depth help to their older clients as one reason for starting out in this field.

Those just graduating from pharmacy school should be able to get help locating jobs through their schools' placement offices. Professional organizations are also sources of information; the American Society of Consultant Pharmacists provides a listing of companies that hire recent graduates as well as employment listings on its website.

Graduates can also apply to and complete residency programs in geriatric pharmacy. Such a residency will give you further training for working in this field and enhance your credentials. The American

Society of Health-System Pharmacists offers several residencies, including residencies in pharmacy practice and residencies in geriatric pharmacy. During a residency, which usually lasts one year, pharmacists work full time and earn a stipend. Residents who complete their programs have excellent employment prospects. Sometimes they are offered jobs at the places of their residencies.

Another option is, like Lenart, to begin working in a pharmacy that provides services to a general population, gain work experience, and move into geriatric pharmacy practice when the opportunity presents itself.

ADVANCEMENT

Senior care pharmacists can advance by moving to larger pharmacies for more responsibilities, such as managing a larger staff of pharmacy technicians and working with more nursing facilities than they had in their past jobs. Other senior care pharmacists may consider it an advancement to move into a different area of consulting, for example, changing from nursing facility consulting to long-term care facility consulting. Those in academia advance by becoming full professors, and those in industry may advance by obtaining positions with increased management responsibilities. Some senior care pharmacists with experience may decide to form their own consulting businesses, either alone or in partnership with other pharmacists.

EARNINGS

According to Ward Lenart, salaries for senior care pharmacists are generally on par with what other pharmacists earn. He does note, though, that "some pharmacies view [senior care pharmacists] as a sort of sales/representative in addition to their duties as pharmacists." In these cases, senior care pharmacists are usually at the higher end of the pay scale. Other factors that influence salaries include location and type of employer and the pharmacist's experience.

According to the U.S. Department of Labor, pharmacists had median yearly incomes of $77,050 in 2002. The department also reported that the lowest paid 10 percent earned less than $54,110, while the highest paid 10 percent made more than $94,570 annually.

Pharmacists, in addition to salary, often enjoy fringe benefits such as paid vacation time, medical and dental insurance, retirement plans, and sometimes bonuses, depending on the size and type of employer.

WORK ENVIRONMENT

Pharmacies must be clean and orderly as well as well lighted and well ventilated. They are frequently busy places and this is especially true for those serving a large number of geriatric patients, since older people often take more than one medication at a time. In addition to working in a pharmacy, senior care pharmacists also visit their patients and consult with other members of the patient's health care team. This means there is a certain amount of travel involved in the senior care pharmacist's work. Additionally, because these pharmacists are in contact with such a variety of people, from elderly people in pain to concerned family members to other health care professionals, they may often need to be diplomatic when advising on why and how medications should be taken.

The two most unfavorable conditions of the pharmacist's practice are the long hours and the necessity to stay on one's feet. Most state laws covering the practice of pharmacy require that there be a pharmacist on duty at all times when a pharmacy is open. This may mean long shifts as, for example, hospital pharmacies are continuously open. Despite these factors, most senior care pharmacists appreciate being involved in health care where they can use their medical and scientific knowledge to help older patients feel better.

Those who run their own businesses have management and financial responsibilities. They must hire employees, keep records on patients, and keep track of costs. They must make rent or mortgage payments and pay insurance premiums and taxes.

OUTLOOK

The U.S. Department of Labor predicts that job opportunities for pharmacists will grow faster than the average through 2012. The number of available positions is expected to exceed the number of people entering the field, mainly due to pharmacists who are retiring or otherwise leaving the field. Although the U.S. Department of Labor does not provide an employment outlook specifically for senior care pharmacists, it does cite the growing elderly population in the United States as a reason for the good job prospects for pharmacists. Senior citizens are expected to take an increasing number of prescription medications as a result of continuing medical advances and new drug research.

The demand for pharmacists in hospitals will not be as great as other areas of the industry, since hospitals are increasing the amount of outpatient visits and decreasing the length of patient stays; this prompts people to purchase prescriptions from other retail venues, such as drug store and supermarket pharmacies, where job outlooks will be quite good. Other avenues for geriatric pharmacists include working for pharmaceutical manufacturing companies, especially those that manufacture drugs designed to treat ailments that affect senior citizens. In such contexts, pharmacists can work in research and development, or even in the marketing and advertising of new drug products.

FOR MORE INFORMATION

For more information on accredited programs, visit the ACPE website.
American Council on Pharmaceutical Education (ACPE)
20 North Clark Street, Suite 2500
Chicago, IL 60602-5109
Tel: 312-664-3575
http://www.acpe-accredit.org

For more information about senior care pharmacists contact
American Society of Consultant Pharmacists
1321 Duke Street
Alexandria, VA 22314-3563
Tel: 800-355-2727
Email: info@ascp.com
http://ascp.com

The ASHSP has information on geriatric program residencies and news of interest for those in long-term care.
American Society of Health-System Pharmacists (ASHSP)
7272 Wisconsin Avenue
Bethesda, MD 20814
Tel: 301-657-3000
http://www.ashp.org

For information about certification, contact
Commission for Certification in Geriatric Pharmacy
1321 Duke Street
Alexandria, VA 22314
Tel: 703-535-3038
http://www.ccgp.org

––––––––––– **INTERVIEW** –––––––––––

Michael Chudyk, Pharm.D., has been a licensed pharmacist since 1984. He is currently a senior staff pharmacist at Saint Vincent's

Hospital in New York City. He recently joined a pharmacy consulting group where he works part time with the long-term care industry, specifically covering four nursing homes in Manhattan and Brooklyn. He spoke with the editors of Careers in Focus: Geriatric Care *about his career.*

Q. What made you decide to become a pharmacist?

A. It was a fascination with how something as miniscule as a tablet or capsule could have such a profound effect on a human being or animal. I was also interested in learning more about anatomy, physiology, biochemistry, and other related science subjects and the interplay among them and to see how this translated into medications, vitamins, or herbs mimicking, negating, or augmenting bodily functions. Becoming a pharmacist would also provide an opportunity to help people by answering their questions about medical conditions, diseases, and medications, recommending over-the-counter treatments and referring people to appropriate medical care.

Q. What attracted you to the field of geriatrics?

A. My father suffered a very disabling stroke in 1988 and is still alive today and cared for at home by our family. This has made me realize that because of increasing life expectancies in this country, there are many older people living independent and productive lives while often dealing with several concurrent diseases, such as hypertension, elevated cholesterol, arthritis, osteoporosis, Alzheimer's disease, and depression, just to name a few. In the United States today, there are more than 50,000 people age 100 or over, and that number is projected to reach 1 million by 2050. The 85+ age group is the fastest growing segment of the U.S. population, and it is the segment that is more likely to consume medications for the treatment of different disease states. With more than 10,000 medications on the market, many with specific dosing requirements or drug interactions, understanding when or how to take medications can get pretty confusing. Add to this the elderly patient's declining senses (hearing, eyesight, etc.), and the potential for problems is obvious.

Being a geriatric pharmacist presents an interesting and challenging opportunity to manage various disease states and see the difference this makes in a patient's life. In addition, despite the increasing size of the elderly population, specialists in geriatrics, such as geriatric physicians and geriatric pharmacists, are still in the minority in their professions.

Q. What sort of education and training did you receive for your career? Did you undertake any special courses of study to specialize in geriatric pharmacy?

A. I have a bachelor of science degree in pharmacy and a doctor of pharmacy degree, both from St. John's University. The doctor of pharmacy is a six-year program of study and is becoming the entry-level pharmacy degree for all U.S. pharmacy schools. I also earned a master's degree in business administration from Manhattan College.

In order to develop a stronger background in geriatrics, I supplemented my work experience by receiving board certification as a certified geriatric pharmacist. I also maintain my skills and knowledge through my membership in professional societies such as the American Society of Consultant Pharmacists, by reading professional publications, and by attending continuing education programs.

Q. What would you say are the pros and cons of your career?

A. The workload and stress of being a pharmacist can be overwhelming at times. Although the compensation is quite competitive regardless of where one practices (annual starting salaries of $100,000 are fairly common) and job opportunities are abundant, the hours can be quite long.

Q. What would you say are the most important skills and personal qualities for all pharmacists?

A. Some important skills are the ability to work well and accurately under pressure, to think analytically and to know how to delegate responsibilities and recognize and solve problems. Important personal qualities include patience and understanding, the ability to foster relationships and command trust, and the ability to hold oneself to high ethical standards.

Q. What sort of unique challenges does being a senior care pharmacist present?

A. Older patients present unique characteristics. They will likely have age-related impairments in hearing, vision, and taste, and they may require more time and a little bit of patience when discussing their medical concerns or understanding your instructions or recommendations.

Q. What advice would you give to someone who is interested in pursuing this type of career? How might one start to prepare for a career as a pharmacist?

A. Prepare well academically, especially in the sciences (specifically chemistry) and math, since these subjects are heavily emphasized in the pharmacy curriculum. The program of study leading to the doctor of pharmacy degree is lengthy (six years) and competitive (it's not uncommon to see class sizes shrink each year due to attrition). The entire six years of study can be demanding, with semesters entailing 16–18 credits and days running from 8:00 A.M. to 5:00 P.M., not including assignments. So you have to be committed to this kind of undertaking.

Getting involved with extracurricular activities (e.g., leadership roles in student pharmacy organizations) and working in a pharmacy setting (preferably various settings, to get a better sense of different organizations) are also helpful in fostering professional development.

There is a considerable investment of time and money in becoming a pharmacist, but the rewards that follow usually more than make up for this, as does the security of having a lucrative, challenging, and rewarding career.

Index

Entries and page numbers in **bold** indicate major treatment of a topic.